Kitten Cupid

Also by Anna Wilson

Kitten Kaboodle
Kitten Smitten

Puppy Love
Pup Idol
Puppy Power

And chosen by Anna Wilson

Fairy Stories
Princess Stories

Anna Wilson

Kitten Cupid

Illustrated by MOIRA MUNRO

MACMILLAN CHILDREN'S BOOKS

First published 2010 by Macmillan Children's Books
a division of Macmillan Publishers Limited
20 New Wharf Road, London N1 9RR
Basingstoke and Oxford
Associated companies throughout the world
www.panmacmillan.com

ISBN 978-0-330-51832-1

1 3 5 7 9 8 6 4 2

A CIP catalogue record for this book is available from the British Library.

Printed and bound in the UK by CPI Mackays, Chatham ME5 8TD

For Lucy
Good luck in September!
With all my love

1

New Beginnings

After the summer when my (very own!) cute little ginger kitten, Jaffa, won a TV talent show, *Pets with Talent*, and my best mate, Jazz got to meet her idol, Danni Minnow, you would think that life could only be described as totally mega-fantastically excellent. And it was – for the rest of that summer. In fact, when I looked back, I could hardly believe I was the same Bertie Fletcher as the year before. So much had changed, and in such a short space of time.

Not only had my previously non-pet-loving dad fallen completely head over heels for my new kitten, but Jazz and I had patched up the worrying

cracks that had been appearing in our friendship. And we had a new friend, Fergus Meerley. (Not a great name, I know, but you can't have everything.) He and his parents, Fiona and Gavin, moved into our neighbour Pinkella's house when she had to go away. Between you and me, his mum was a bit of a pain in the neck to start with. (Actually, that's an understatement. Make that a TOTAL AND UTTER pain in every single part of the body you can think of.) She persuaded Jaffa to move in with them and made out it was because she thought my kitten was an *abandoned stray*! But she more than paid for her 'mistake' by sorting out the *Pets with Talent* show that Danni Minnow judged. And Jazz was made up about that, I can tell you!

Anyway, it was worth putting up with someone like Fiona because without her I wouldn't have met Fergus. (*Yes*, he's a boy, but he's cool, all right? Not only does he love animals as much as I do, he's also an amazing musician.)

So, you might be forgiven for thinking that by the end of the summer all my worries were dead and buried. But I am a natural worrier, so I was still left agonizing over the next thing on the horizon: senior school. And that was a worry which would *not* go away, no matter how much Jazz and Fergus tried to reassure me.

'I just don't get what you're so uptight about,' Jazz said one afternoon when the two of us were lounging around on rugs in my back garden. We had been idly watching Jaffa chase butterflies when I'd suddenly realized how little freedom we had left.

'I can't WAIT to start school!' Jazz chirruped, pushing herself up on one elbow and grinning at me. 'It's going to be, like, *immense*! For starters, I'll be getting the bus instead of having to go in the car with my complete earwig of a brother. Oh wow, just think – no more Tyson coming up to me at break time with snotty tears running down his face because someone's "been nasty" to him; no more Tyson calling out annoying insults to me in the lunch queue. Hey, just NO MORE TYSON, actually!'

'But aren't you nervous about starting at a new place?' I asked.

'Nervous? What's to be nervous about?' Jazz sounded puzzled.

'Well, you know – finding your way around the place, loads of difficult homework, new teachers who might turn out to be freaks. That kind of thing,' I babbled, avoiding mentioning what was really at the front of my mind.

'Oh, Bertie!' Jazz said, her voice oozing pity all of a sudden, making me squirm. 'We're not the only new ones, are we? And we've had that induction day already, when they showed us around. I bet they'll even get some of the older guys to look out for us.'

Exactly, I thought. A picture flitted into my

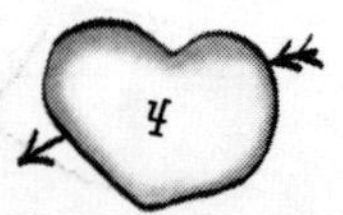

harassed mind of my best mate joking and flirting with a load of older pupils – maybe even some of the guys in Fergus's year.

'I guess,' I said reluctantly, rolling on to my back and staring at the clouds. 'But what if . . .' I tailed off.

Jazz peered at me encouragingly. 'Yeah? What if what?'

I rolled over on to my front again so she couldn't see my face, took a deep breath and let the words come out in a rush: 'What if you make a whole load of super-cool new friends and don't want to have anything to do with me any more?'

Jazz tutted and flung a long skinny arm around my shoulders. 'Doh! You numpty! What would I want to do that for?'

I felt a mixture of embarrassment and relief flood through me as my best mate gave me a squeeze. 'Dunno,' I grunted, shrugging.

'Is that it? Is that what you're really worried

about?' Jazz said. 'Me abandoning you, my best friend in the whole world? As if!'

'Sorry, you're right,' I said, turning to look at her from under my fringe. 'But, er . . . what about Fergus?'

'What *about* Fergus?' Jazz prompted. There was an edge to her voice now.

She was getting impatient with me.

'Oh, nothing,' I said. 'Want an ice pop?'

I wished I hadn't mentioned Fergus. Jazz had teased me about him a bit recently, saying she thought I fancied him, and I didn't want to give her the chance to start that again. How could I explain to her that I really liked him. *That was all.* I didn't want anyone thinking it was 'like that' between us. I could just picture Jazz in one of her gossipy moods letting slip one day to someone that she thought it was more than that. Boy, that would be sooooo embarrassing.

My kitten saw me leaving the garden and stopped chasing bees and butterflies to pad along

behind me and Jazz, following us into the kitchen. She never liked being far from me these days.

'Whassup?' she mewed.

I whirled round and scooped her up to face height. 'Ssh, Jaffsie,' I whispered. 'Can't talk now with Jazz here.'

(And before you go thinking I've well and truly lost my marbles, yes, I can talk to my cat. But my friends and family don't know about it, so please don't tell anyone; just go with me on this, OK?)

'Hey, you talking to your little puddy tat again, Bertie?' Jazz teased, flinging open the freezer door. 'You really love that cat, don't you?'

'Mmm, I sure do!' I grinned, rubbing my face against my kitten's whiskery cheek.

Her purring went up a notch and I giggled as her fur tickled me.

'Awww,' said Jazz, watching us. 'You're going to miss your Bertie when she goes back to school, aren't you, diddums?'

'Cut out the baby talk, can't you, Jazz?' I said. I knew it probably sounded weird to Jazz, my talking to my kitten like I did to a person instead of the usual way people talked to their pets, but it irritated me that Jazz took the mickey. Why shouldn't I talk to my pet how I wanted? I hated all that 'pussy-wussy-cat-kins' nonsense I heard from other cat owners.

'Whoooo! OK, keep *cool*, man!' Jazz guffawed, waving an ice pop at me while tearing open another with her teeth.

I couldn't help sniggering at Jazz's lame joke. But I stopped mid-giggle when Jaffa said:

'What is the Jazzer talkin' 'bout, Bertie? What is "school"?'

My throat went dry. I hadn't told Jaffa I'd be going to school! She had come to live with me at the beginning of the summer holidays so as far as she was concerned I was at home all the time, day in, day out, 24-7. The longest I'd ever left her was

to pop out to Jazz's house or to go and see Fergus. And now I was about to leave her from breakfast until teatime, five days a week. She would freak, wouldn't she? I would have to break it to her gently.

'Earth calling Bertie!' Jazz was jeering, waving a hand in my face and laughing. 'What's happened to you? Turned into a statue or something?'

I blinked and tried to push my increasingly panicky thoughts to the back of my mind. 'Oh, ha ha ha!' I chuckled unconvincingly. 'Sorry, went off into a bit of a dream there for a second!'

'Bertieeeeeee!' Jaffa mewed. 'Tell Jaffsie what is happening! Tell Jaffsie what the "school" thing is!'

'Blimey, Jaffa,' I said, frantically trying to distract my kitten. 'You *are* making a racket. Are you hungry?'

'Noooooo!' Jaffa howled. 'Me wants you to tell meeeeee—'

'So did you hear what I said just then?' Jazz raised her voice to talk over the rumpus Jaffa was making. She raised one eyebrow at me and slurped loudly on her ice pop. The red colouring was already leaking around the edges of her mouth.

I must have looked blank, because Jazz rolled her eyes and, taking the ice pop out of her mouth, she said in a sing-song tone, 'What are you going to do while you're at school?' When I didn't respond she persisted: 'Will Jaffa be OK on her own here all day? Or will your dad be working at home the whole time?'

I started mouthing at Jazz to stop talking, and when that didn't work I threw myself into a loud coughing fit in desperation.

'Whaaaat?' Jaffa positively shrieked. 'Bertie is going to leave Jaffsie ALL DAY?'

Holy Stromboli with mushrooms and extra cheese on top – as if it wasn't bad enough being worried about starting a new school! Now I had a hysterical kitten on my hands.

How on earth was I going to get out of this one?

2

Cat-Sitter Wanted

Eventually, when she could see she wasn't going to get anywhere with me, Jazz let the whole Jaffa thing drop and moved on to jabbering about the stuff we needed for school. She also wanted to run through our plans for the first morning for about the millionth time that week. Jazz was going to wait for me and Fergus at the bus stop, and we would hopefully all sit together. I was relieved about that. I didn't much like the idea of getting the bus on my own with all the older kids.

Jaffa wasn't so easily thrown off the scent though. She prowled around, listening in and constantly nudging my arm with her fluffy little head, asking me what we were talking about. Not for the first time she reminded me of Jazz's little brother, Tyson, who had no concept of personal space and would get right in between me and Jazz and practically tread on our toes so that he could get bang in the middle of a conversation we were having.

I decided that the best policy was the one I often had to adopt with Ty, which was to ignore Jaffa's interruptions, and thankfully she finally gave up mewing and pawing at me and fell asleep on the rug on her back, her paws in the air as though she'd just fallen out of an aeroplane and landed like that, back legs outstretched and front paws up above her. It was a pose she was adopting more and more these days, and it usually made me want to tickle her tummy. But this time I was so grateful to be finally left in peace that I

resisted the temptation.

Jazz had to go home soon after that, and I saw her out, leaving Jaffa snoozing on the rug. As I closed the front door Dad came out of his study.

'Oh, Jazz gone?' he asked. 'That's a shame. Thought she might like to stay for supper. I was going to do pizza tonight. Bex is coming round.'

'Right,' I said.

'You don't mind, do you?' Dad asked, coming down the stairs and eyeing me anxiously.

I sighed. How could I say I minded? It wasn't that Bex wasn't nice. She'd been a great help with Jaffa when we'd first got her, and she was always friendly to me. She owned the pet shop in town, Paws for Thought: Dad and I had met her when we first got Jaffa and needed advice on what to feed her and so on. Bex was crazy about animals, as you'd expect from someone who owned a pet shop, and she had a cheeky Border terrier called Sparky, who came to work with her and sat in a sweet little bed at the foot of the counter, wagging his tail at anyone who came in. In any other circumstances I would have been over the moon to get to know a person who owned such a cool shop and such a friendly pooch. But the thing was, *Dad* was even more interested in getting to know Bex than I was, if you see what I mean. And I wasn't sure I was ready for my dad to get himself a girlfriend. You know what they say: two's company, three's a crowd . . .

'It's just pizza!' Dad laughed awkwardly, noting the look of distaste on my face.

'Yeah, whatever,' I said hastily. I didn't really want him to go into any more details.

'You OK, love?' he asked, giving me a hug. 'You seem a bit down in the dumps for someone who's just spent a lovely summer's day outside with her best mate and her favourite kitten!' he added. He was trying to sound jolly and light-hearted.

I found myself getting increasingly irritated

with every word that came out of his mouth.

'Yeah, yeah, I'm fine, all right? I'm going to feed Jaffsie,' I said sullenly. I shrugged his arm from my shoulder. A little voice inside me was telling me not to be so mean to him, but I couldn't help it.

I stomped sulkily towards the garden, intending to call Jaffa in, but Dad wouldn't let it go.

'Bertie,' he said, following me out, 'if you've got a problem, you know you can talk to me. Have you and Jazz had one of your, er, fallings-out?' he asked nervously.

'No!' I spluttered. 'Really, it's nothing.'

'Well, it doesn't look like nothing to me,' he persisted.

That was it. Something inside me snapped, and everything I'd been silently battling with that afternoon came out in a rush.

'OK!' I said harshly, throwing my hands up in the air. 'You want to know what's bugging me? It's this: I don't want to go to school. I don't want to go to a big new school where I hardly know anyone and where I'm going to have to be bottom of the pile again – one of the babies.' I hesitated, gulping for air. 'And I . . . and I don't want to leave Jaffa at home every day!' My voice rose in a squeak and a hot pricking sensation rose up behind my eyes. I blinked hard. I was *not* going to cry.

Dad frowned and then bit his bottom lip. He looked as though he was trying to decide whether to tell me off for being rude to him or give me a big bear hug and reassure me things would turn out OK.

In the end he said softly, 'Bertie, I wish you'd talk to me before you go and make everything so complicated for yourself.' He shook his head slightly and looked at me sadly. 'I was your age once too, you know.'

I rolled my eyes. Yeah, yeah. About a hundred years ago, I thought bitterly. But I just said, 'You weren't a *girl* though, were you, Dad?'

'Not as far as I remember,' Dad said, a cheeky grin breaking through his worried expression. Then his eyes lit up and I saw he was having one of his light-bulb moments. My stomach did a somersault as I realized even before he opened his mouth what he was going to say.

'No, Dad!' I said hastily, waving my hands in front of his eager puppy-dog face. 'No, no, no. I am *not* going to talk to Bex about this.' Dad was always trying to make up for the fact that I didn't have a mum. (Any more, that is. She died when I was small.)

Dad blushed and said, 'I was only going to say—'

'I know what you were going to say: that Bex, being a girl – woman, whatever – might be a good person to talk to. Well, I don't want to.'

Dad opened his mouth to reply, but then, as if on cue, the doorbell rang.

'That'll be her,' Dad said, blushing a deeper red and flicking his eyes towards the door. 'Look,

I promise I won't embarrass you, OK? But don't go to your room, Bertie – stay and have pizza with us?'

I gritted my teeth.

The doorbell rang again, and Dad shot me a pleading look and went into the house to let Bex in.

I followed, wondering whether I should ignore Dad's request and go to my room anyway, when my thoughts were interrupted by Jaffa, who came skittering down the hall so fast her little legs were flying out at all angles.

'Is it Jaffsie's teatime yet?' she mewed breathlessly. 'Jaffsie was sleepin', then me hears that ringy bell thing goin'. Where's the Jazzer gone? Oh!' she said, skidding to a halt as she saw Bex standing in the doorway, greeting Dad, all shiny smile and sparkly teeth and glittery everything. Urgh. 'It's the lovely Bexy lady!' Jaffa purred, trotting up to her and rubbing her head against her legs.

'Hello, Bertie!' Bex beamed. 'And hello, little darling!' she cooed, bending down to stroke Jaffa.

'Thought you were talking to me for a moment there,' Dad said in a goofy voice.

'Oh, Nigel! Tee-hee! You are a silly billy!' Bex trilled, tittering in that annoying way she always did whenever she spoke to Dad.

'Yes, Bertie's dad *very* silly. Me is the only darling around here,' Jaffa muttered grumpily.

I let my head sink back and stared at the ceiling in despair. How was I going to survive this evening?

Jaffa was up on her hind legs now, pawing at Bex and begging for a cuddle.

'Someone's pleased to see me!' Bex twittered, picking Jaffa up and nuzzling her. 'Good job I didn't bring Sparky. Otherwise you might change your mind, mightn't you, you gorgeous little thing?' she went on.

Jaffa was purring so loudly she sounded more

like a contented puma than a small ginger kitten. 'You is so right – me is totally gorgeous,' she said.

'Doh!' I let out an exasperated breath and stomped off to the kitchen, thinking I might as well leave the three of them out there to enjoy their mutual love fest.

'Bertie!' Dad called. 'Can you lay the table out in the garden? There's a love.'

I crashed around the kitchen, getting what I needed, and then went out on to the patio, practically throwing plates and cutlery at the table in my fury. How dare that woman be such a flirt with my dad – not to *mention* with my kitten! My mind was whirring with so many confused and angry thoughts that I didn't hear anyone come outside.

'Er, are you all right, Bertie?'

I looked up sharply. Great. Dad had sent Bex out to check on me. I glared at her. She was holding a very pleased-with-herself Jaffa in her arms.

'Only,' Bex went on tentatively, 'you seem a

bit – cross?' She waited, but I didn't say anything. 'D'you want me to go?'

'Nooooo!' Jaffa whined. 'Jaffsie not want the lovely Bexy lady to goooo!'

Well, Bertie does! I thought. But I couldn't say that, could I? Dad would be livid.

I settled for a shrug instead.

Bex looked intensely uncomfortable. 'Your dad and I . . .' She stalled. 'We're not, erm, seeing each other or anything, you know. What I mean is, we're just friends, that's all.'

I chewed the inside of my mouth and went back to glaring at her.

Jaffa had started wriggling in Bex's arms, I noticed gratifyingly. Bex set her down gently on the grass and ploughed on: 'I mean, I really like your dad. As in, really, *really* like him. But I want you to know there's no way I'd ever come between you and him.'

'Bertieeee,' Jaffa complained, rubbing against

my ankles, 'me is staaaarvin''.'

But I wasn't listening to Jaffa. Despite the churning in my heart, something about what Bex was saying had shifted the dark feelings deep inside me, and I found myself softening slightly. I felt bad all of a sudden; it wasn't Bex's fault that I was in such a mood.

'I hope you don't me saying,' Bex said, taking a step towards me, 'but your dad said you're anxious about starting at senior school.'

'What *is* "school"?' Jaffa pestered.

I scooped her up and hissed, 'Be quiet.' Then I looked at Bex and nodded.

Bex smiled and pulled back a chair. She sat down and looked up at me while I shuffled my feet and stared at the paving stones. 'It's always tough starting something new,' she said quietly. 'I was scared stiff when I started in Year Seven – not that it was called that back in the Dark Ages!' She laughed. 'And I was terrified on my first day of college – and

on the first day of my first job . . .' She paused.

I looked up at her. 'Really?' I said hoarsely.

'Of course!' she said. 'There aren't many people who don't get flustered by change.'

'Jazz doesn't,' I mumbled, hiding my face in Jaffa's fur.

Bex put her head on one side. 'Is that what's bothering you?' she asked.

I shrugged again.

'Are you worried that Jazz is excited about school and you're not?'

I pulled a face. 'Dunno. Maybe.'

Jaffa had started wriggling again, so I put her down and fiddled with the knives and forks on the table.

'What is you doin', Bertie?' Jaffa mewed. 'Me wants teeeeeeea!' I bent down and whispered into her tiny triangle of an ear, 'OK! OK!' Then I turned to Bex. 'I just have to feed her.'

I went to the utility room, leaving Bex outside,

and roughly dished up Jaffa's food. 'Listen,' I said to her, 'we're eating too in a minute. Are you going to be good and sit quietly with us?'

'Uh-huh,' Jaffa mewed. She set to gobbling up her meal as if I hadn't fed her in weeks.

I went back out to the garden to find Bex standing, arms folded, looking at me thoughtfully and saying nothing. I tried to avoid her gaze and wished I could think of something to say to break the awkward atmosphere.

Thankfully Jaffa provided a distraction by appearing in the doorway and mewling, 'Me done now – can me have a special Bertie cuddle?'

I picked her up gently and she licked my cheek with her pink sandpaper tongue.

Suddenly Bex commented, 'I suppose it's always tough going back after the summer anyway. And you've had a

pretty special summer, what with getting gorgeous little Jaffsie – and then being on television as well! No wonder you don't want to go to school . . . Hey! What's the matter?'

I couldn't help it. Those rough little kitten kisses, together with the reminder that I was going to have to leave Jaffa all day, just set me off, and tears were trickling down my hot cheeks. Jaffa started licking at the tears, miaowing pitifully.

Bex pushed her chair back. The metal legs made a harsh scraping noise on the flagstones. I had my head buried in Jaffa's fur now and my shoulders were shaking. I felt Bex put an arm round me and heard her mutter soothing words. She gently pushed me down into a chair and drew one up beside me.

'Come on, Bertie. Tell me what's going on,' she whispered. She took Jaffa from me and stroked her so that she stopped mewing and fell into one of her instant snoozes. Boy, I wished I could do that sometimes.

I gulped and sniffed and tried to swallow my sobs and gradually managed to calm myself down enough to explain how worried I was about leaving Jaffa after what had happened with Fiona Meerley earlier in the summer.

Bex listened patiently. Meanwhile Dad came out into the garden with the pizzas and a bottle of wine for him and Bex and lemonade for me. He exchanged a questioning glance with Bex and sat down quietly opposite me.

At last I stopped talking.

'Well,' said Bex, sitting back in her chair and taking a sip from her glass, 'I can see why you've been getting so upset.'

Dad busied himself with slicing the pizzas and handing them round.

'You know, I think I might have an idea of how I could help though,' Bex said carefully.

I looked at her from under my untidy fringe. 'Yeah?' I caught Dad giving Bex the tiniest nod

and wondered what they were up to. A soft evening breeze washed over me, cooling my warm cheeks.

'I was just thinking,' Bex said airily, 'I mean, it's only an idea, but say your dad has to go out while you're at school . . . well, my shop's not a million miles away, so how would it be if I dropped in on Jaffa throughout the day – just to check she was all right?'

I couldn't believe it. Why would she want to do that? 'But you couldn't,' I protested. 'You'd have to shut the shop.'

Bex stuck out her bottom lip and shook her head. 'No – I've got someone who comes in to help out every so often: Ruth. She's a good friend. She'd be more than happy to stand in for me while I nip out. I'd only be away briefly anyway – just to give Jaffsie a quick cuddle and make sure she's OK. It's not like I'd be away from the shop for hours at a time.'

Dad was beaming at me. He took a huge bite

of his pizza and nodded encouragingly.

It did sound like a good plan, I had to admit. There was still a niggling doubt in me about Bex and what her motives were where Dad was concerned, but I couldn't exactly complain if she was willing to give up her own time to help me out with Jaffa.

'What about Sparky?' I asked.

'He'll be all right in the shop – Ruth can look after him,' Bex said.

I took a long slug of the cold lemonade. Dad looked at me, waiting for me to say something. I put the glass down on the table and said, 'Well, thanks, Bex. If you're sure. It would make it easier for me to leave Jaffsie, I guess.'

'That's that, then!' said Dad, in a satisfied tone. 'More pizza, anyone?'

3

Famous Already

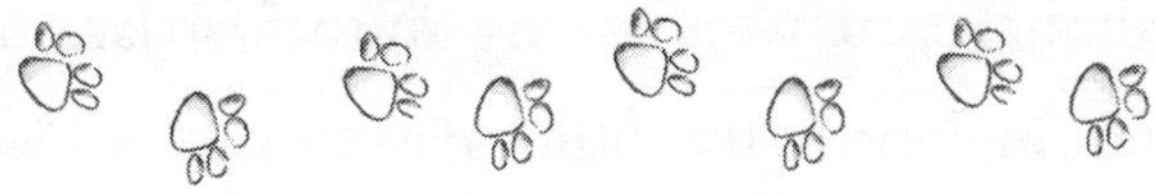

Jaffa had been asleep the whole time Bex was outlining her offer, so it fell to me to explain to my kitten what would happen while I was at school all day. I was worried about telling her about the plan, and only finally plucked up enough courage to talk to her the night before school started. As it turned out, she didn't seem bothered at all.

'Hey, Jaffsie. You sleeping?' I whispered.

'Nah,' Jaffa said, opening one eye. 'Me is just havin' a little snoozette. Not the same as a sleep, cos me can still hear Bertie talkin',' she said. The tone of self-importance in her tiny kitten-voice made me giggle as always.

At the sound of me laughing she opened her other eye and shot me an offended look, so I bit down on my lip and made myself continue: 'Remember you were asking me what Jazz and I were talking about the other day?' I said.

Jaffa stood up and arched her back, and then sat down on her haunches, stretching out luxuriously after her 'snoozette'. 'Mmmm,' she purred in answer.

I gave her a scratch behind the ears, which she leaned into, her pretty mouth turned up into a smile. 'We-ell,' I said hesitantly, screwing up my courage, 'tomorrow after breakfast I am going to school with Jazz, and I won't be back until teatime. School is where children have to go to learn things,' I added.

She interrupted me: 'But Jaffsie will not be alone. Bertie's dad is here.'

'Ye-es,' I ploughed on, smiling lopsidedly. 'But not all the time. He has a meeting tomorrow in

town, so he'll be out during the day too. But you remember Dad's, er, friend who came over the other night – Bex?' I added swiftly, noting the wide-eyed look of alarm that was spreading over my kitten's fluffy features.

'Mmm,' Jaffa mewed anxiously.

'Well, how would you like it if she looked after you?' I said in a rush.

'*What* is you sayin'?' Jaffa asked. 'Bertie is not giving Jaffsie to the Bexy lady to go and live in another house, is she?'

'No!' I half laughed, to cover the lurching feeling in my stomach. 'No, of course not. Bex would just pop in and check on you while Dad's out, and then I'll be back for tea, and you and I can spend loads of time together in the evening.'

'Oh, OK!' she said. 'So . . . Bertie is going to a place called "school" all day to learn things which is borin', and Jaffsie is going to stay at home with the lovely Bexy lady until Bertie comes back,' Jaffa mewed happily.

'Er, yes. That's more or less it,' I said grumpily.

'So what is the problem?' Jaffa asked, leaping on to my desk, where I had been setting out my *new* stationery before packing it in my *new* bag. 'Why does Bertie sound so sad?'

'I thought *you'd* be sad, what with me leaving you all day,' I muttered.

'Oh no, Jaffsie won't be sad. Jaffsie not alone. Me has got Bertie's dad and the lovely Bexy lady,' she chattered, walking over my notebooks and batting my pencils about with her small paws.

I whisked her into the air with one hand and held her close to my face. 'Well, just so you are clear about this,' I said softly, '*Bertie* is sad about leaving Jaffsie. So you'd better not get any ideas into your head about going off to live anywhere else. It was bad enough the first time,' I said meaningfully.

If a cat could blush, I would have said that's what Jaffa did in response. She flicked her ears

back and turned her head away from me, squeaking indignantly. 'Me was a tiny very young kitten then. Me didn't know Bertie was my owner. Me has learned my lessons now me is all growed up,' she said in a hurt tone.

'Pleased to hear it,' I whispered, stroking her head with my free hand. 'Cos you know what? I don't know what I'd do without you.'

Jazz had already texted me before I'd opened my eyes the next morning. I could see the red light flashing on my phone when I staggered over to where it had been plugged in to charge overnight.

I flicked open the screen and scrolled through to the messages while I stepped out of my pyjamas and fished a clean pair of pants out of my top drawer.

Hey! r u up yet? c u at bus ☺ x

Just reading that little text had sent a wave of relief gushing through me. Thank goodness for Jazz.

How could I feel nervous when I had my best mate to look out for me?

Then I noticed the time in the top right-hand corner of the small screen – seven thirty! Why hadn't Dad knocked on my door? I was going to miss the bus altogether! Then what would I do? Jazz would get there before me and would have memorized the names of everyone in our class; she would have sussed out (in her words) 'who was hot and who was not', and I would arrive late, sweaty and flustered . . .

I scrambled into my new uniform, trying to get my feet into the gross tights we had to wear without laddering them. At my old school we'd been allowed to wear trousers, but this one made the lower-school girls wear skirts. I was going to look so *sad* and so . . . *new*. My heart plummeted into my squeaky shiny *new* shoes.

I was sure Jazz would already have found a way to make the uniform look cool, but personally I

couldn't imagine how she would do it. But then I've never had much imagination when it comes to clothes. Just a jeans and T-shirt girl, that's me.

'Dad,' I yelled, bowling into the kitchen at top speed, still raking a brush through my hair, 'why didn't you wake me? It's my first day!'

Dad looked up from his newspaper and frowned over the top of his glasses. 'I *did* wake you – about twenty minutes ago!' he said sternly. 'I thought you were in the shower. Blimey, Bertie. Your hair looks like a half-built birds' nest. You can't start your new school looking like that! And the bus leaves in—'

'I know, I KNOW, all right?' I cried, pulling even harder on my hairbrush. My hair was always a nightmare. It was supposed to be curly, but more often than not it was just a mess: it was the kind of hair that reacted to outside influences beyond my control, like the weather or how hot the central heating was. It was my own personal barometer. Lucky me. 'I haven't got time for a lecture!' I shrieked as I tugged too hard and pulled a clump of hair out by the roots.

Dad immediately looked as though he regretted laying into me and got up to give me a hug. 'Come and have a piece of toast at least,' he said. 'You need something for breakfast.'

I took a deep breath and sat down at the table. I rummaged through my new school bag, checking for the millionth time to see that I had packed enough pencils, rubbers, notebooks, rulers . . .

WHAT I NEED FOR SCHOOL

New pencils

New pencil case (animal design, but not babyish)

New rubber

New pencil sharpener (~~prefferrabl~~ preferably one that actually works)

New ink pen
(don't forget cartridges)
New ink eraser
New notebook (cover design: see new pencil case above)
New bag (must not be girly in any way)

'You'll be fine,' Dad said completely unconvincingly. He sounded even more anxious than I felt, if that was possible.

He eyed me cautiously, handing me a plate with a slice of toast and jam on it. Then, pouring me a cup of tea and stirring in some sugar, he said, 'I remember feeling nervous on my first day at senior school, you know.' He grinned and stared into the middle distance. 'Course, we didn't have girls at our school. That would have made life a whole lot more complicated.'

'Cheers,' I said sarcastically through a mouthful of toast. I took a huge gulp of tea and then pushed back my chair, wiping my mouth on the sleeve of my new jumper.

'Bertie!' Dad admonished.

'Sorry, gotta go!' I cried, grabbing my bag and making for the door. 'Bus leaves in two minutes and I said I'd meet Jazz.'

'Teeth!' Dad yelled.

'Done them already!' I yelled back, slamming the door behind me. I hadn't, of course, but which was more important: the faint chance that one missed brushing session might cause instant tooth decay, or the much bigger chance that one missed bus would cause instant humiliation and a detention on my first day?

I could see Jazz waiting on the corner, jumping up and down and waving at me manically. Luckily the bus wasn't there yet, but there was a small huddle of kids from the neighbourhood, wearing the same rank grey skirt/trousers/green jumper combo as I was. Jazz, even from a distance, looked a little

different from all the others.

I broke into a run, my new shoes pinching my toes, my new shirt rubbing uncomfortably against my skin . . . and my new skirt riding up my legs, I noted with embarrassment. I tugged it back down only to have it ride back up again. It was clinging to those gross nylon tights. My bag banged against my back and the strap cut into my shoulders.

It wasn't until I was within earshot of Jazz that I realized I hadn't said goodbye to Jaffa. In fact, I hadn't seen her at all that morning. Maybe she had freaked out during the night about me leaving her. Maybe she'd run away after all. Maybe—

'Hey, whassup?' Jazz was shrieking, flinging her arms around me as if the last time she'd seen me had been years, rather than hours, ago. The beads in her hair whipped against my cheeks. 'You look kinda – *stressy*!' She laughed. It was the word she always used to describe me. At least some things never change, I thought, relaxing enough to smile back at my overexcited friend. 'Did you get my text? You didn't reply!'

She let me go and I straightened myself up a bit. 'Yeah, well, you know. Nervous,' I said, shrugging. 'Oh, and I overslept.'

'Just *chillax*!' Jazz said brightly. 'I told you, it'll be fine! It's not like you wanted to go back to that old dump of a junior school, is it? Imagine, Mr Grebe will be doing his usual 'And if I have to say that one more time, young lady' routine, only it'll be someone else getting it in the neck this term, NOT ME!' she shouted, punching the air triumphantly. It was then that I noticed the first thing that made her stand out from all the other newbies. She was wearing a ton of purple bangles on one wrist. I took a good long look at her then, as the bus came into view. The bangles were not the only addition to her outfit. My funky friend had already customized her school bag with stickers and key rings, she had a new set of beads in her hair –

purple, of course, but also black, blue and white – and she'd had her ears pierced!

'Like the earrings,' I said, as I followed her on to the bus.

'Thanks.' Jazz beamed. 'Mum *finally* relented yesterday afternoon when I pointed out that she and Leesh have their ears done, so would she care to elaborate on what *exactly* the huge deal was about *me* having them done?'

I raised my eyebrows. I couldn't quite imagine Jazz putting it like that and getting away with it. Mrs Brown, Jazz's mum, was just as much a force to be reckoned with as her feisty younger daughter. It was more likely that Jazz had nagged and nagged so long and hard that in the end her mum had given in out of sheer exhaustion.

We showed the driver our stiff, shiny new passes and filed down the central aisle, looking for a couple of empty seats so that we could sit together. The bus was already heaving with kids.

I'd taken the bus to our old school enough times when Dad hadn't been able to drive me, so I shouldn't have been freaked out by anything. But somehow when I was one of the 'big girls' in our last school, I at least felt I knew where I belonged. Now, on this crowded bus full of teenagers, I felt small and shy, just as I'd feared I would.

Jazz grabbed my hand and dragged me along behind her.

'Here,' she said. She flung her bag on to the floor and slid across to a window seat.

I plonked myself down next to her and let out the breath I realized I'd been holding. I was sure everyone had been staring at us, checking us out when we'd boarded the bus. Oh great – I was gripped by a sudden panic – had my skirt been hitched into the back of those gross tights? I pulled madly at the fabric just as a voice screeched out:

'Hey, look, guys!' Whoever was speaking was sitting in a seat somewhere behind us. 'It's Jasmeena

and her mate whatshername . . . *Bertie*. You know, they were on the *telly*. At least, they were in the background in that lame *Pets with Whatever* thing . . .'

My heart fluttered. It hadn't occurred to me that people I didn't know would have watched the talent show Jaffa had won. I mean, obviously there would have been thousands of people I didn't know watching it – we knew that from the votes that had poured in – but I hadn't given a moment's thought to anyone from *this* area actually recognizing us.

Jazz beamed with delight and bobbed up over the top of her seat, scanning the bus to see who had shouted out her name.

'Yeaaaah!' said another voice. 'It *is* her.'

I glanced up at my best mate anxiously, but Jazz was still beaming. She caught my eye. 'It's Kezia,' she said. 'You know, Leanne's sister? She's in Year Nine – she might be in Fergus's class. Hey, Kez!' she called, waving her bangle-festooned arm.

I slid further down my seat, cringing. I couldn't help feeling a Year 9 would not think it was cool to be waved at like a loony by a Year 7.

But Jazz was still grinning when she slid back down next to me. 'This is going to be mega,' she said, eyes shining. 'People know who I am! People in *Year Nine* know who I am! Do you reckon this is what it feels like to be famous?'

I pursed my lips. 'Dunno.'

'Hey, Jasmeeeeeeeena!' someone else was calling out now. 'Can I have your autograph?'

Jazz popped up out of her seat again and said, laughing. 'Autographs in the foyer after the show!'

She was lapping it up, and all my fears of her leaving me for a cooler bunch of friends came surging back. But I was distracted out of my depressing thoughts by the welcome sight of a familiar face. Fergus was coming down the aisle, puffing and panting, his blazer falling off one shoulder. I waved and he saw me.

'Hey!' He came closer, beaming. 'Like the hair, – it's wild!'

I felt myself redden. 'Mmm, it's a new look. I call it "The Wrong Side of the Bed Head".'

Fergus laughed. 'Well, look at me – I overslept on my first day, can you believe it? I told Mum to wake me and she said she had! I must have rolled over and gone back to sleep.'

I grinned. 'Sounds familiar.'

Jazz stopped posing for her fans long enough to sit down and notice Fergus. 'Oh, hey, Fergieeeee,' she drawled, waving her fingers at him and batting her eyelashes. 'You going to come and sit on our laps? Hahaha!' she laughed.

Fergus looked sheepish. 'Yeah, looks like I'm too late to grab a seat, doesn't it? Can I perch on the armrest?'

'Sure,' I said.

We chatted all the way to school, oblivious to anyone else for the rest of the journey. We were still nattering as we shuffled off the bus, the noise level around us growing as people spotted mates they hadn't seen all holiday. Girls were shrieking at each other and waving madly, bags were flailing around dangerously, thwacking people in the arms and legs. Boys were shouting and lobbing footballs and throwing mock punches. It was a crazy crush as we inched through the crowds.

Just as Jazz and I were fumbling our way out of the frenzy, Jazz suddenly yelped.

'Ow!' she said, turning on me accusingly. 'Did you just poke me?'

'No!' I cried. 'What would I do that for?'

'Well, *someone* did,' said Jazz grimly, scouting around for the culprit.

I was just about to tell Jazz she must have imagined it when I felt someone push me hard between the shoulder blades, sending me careering into Jazz. As I tried to regain my footing, I heard a snigger.

Jazz skittered to one side, looking nervously over

her shoulder, and nudged me to get me to move quicker. 'Bertieee!' she urged. 'Let's get inside.'

I pushed my way through the jostling hordes and found a space near the front door just as the bell went. I'd lost sight of Fergus. I guessed he must have made his way to the Year 9 classrooms already. I stood there, catching my breath and trying to straighten myself out. Jazz dodged her way towards me.

'Listen,' I said firmly, holding up a hand. I wanted to stop her from getting a word in edgeways first. 'Before you have a go at me, I didn't touch you. And actually someone just pushed me too. I think it was the same person.'

Jazz looked steely eyed. She said with determination, 'I know. Whoever it is had better watch out.' And she pulled me by the arm as she followed the other Year 7s into the lower-school block.

As we made our way through the double glass-fronted doors, I had a nasty feeling that someone was watching us.

4

Cold Comfort

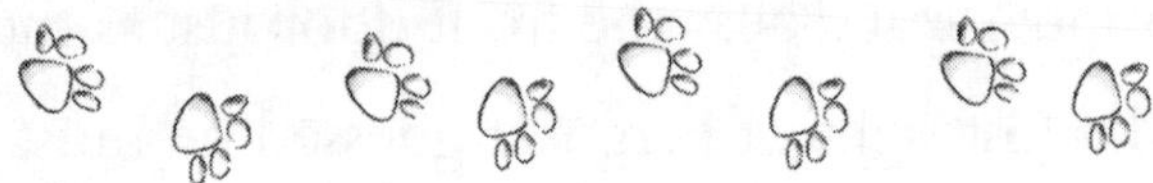

By the time the bell rang for the end of school my mind was whirring with new information and instructions about where to be and when and for how long. (And the homework! *Homework* on our very first day! Can you believe it?) It wasn't until I flopped into a free seat on the bus and closed my eyes for a second that it occurred to me to wonder how Jaffa was doing without me. I immediately felt guilty and hoped and prayed that Bex had not forgotten the poor little cat as well.

I scrambled in my pocket for my phone. We weren't allowed to have our phones with us during school – we had to hand them in to the school

office and collect them at the end of the day. Apparently this changed later in the year, but they had told us that 'New pupils have enough to worry about without losing their phones, iPods and so on,' and so they 'looked after them' for us until we had found our feet. This made me feel like a baby and sent Jazz into one of her huffing-and-puffing routines.

As I turned on my phone I wondered idly where Jazz and Fergus had got to. There had been a mass exodus when the bell had gone, and Jazz and I hadn't been in the same class for last lesson, so I had no idea which direction she'd be coming from. And I hadn't seen Fergus at all since the morning.

My phone beeped and flashed at me. It was a text from Fergus.

Did you have gd day? Mine was gr8! ☺ Have joined band so L8 home. Catch u L8r?

So Fergus was already in with the 'musos' (as he called anyone who was as into music as he was). I was pleased for him as I knew he'd been in a band before he had moved here. He'd told us how gutted he'd been about having to leave his old mates.

I grinned and texted back:

Fab about band! Gotta check on Jaffsie + got tons of h/wk GOL ☹ c u 2moro

I sat back and stared out of the window and my phone beeped again. Maybe Jazz had found out about the band and had stayed to watch them rehearse. That'd be just like her, becoming a groupie on her first day! But it was Bex:

Hope u had nice day. Am at yr house. Will wait for u. Bex x

I couldn't help feeling a bit disappointed. I had hoped Dad would be home to greet me on my first day, not Bex. Still, I supposed it was nice of her not to leave me to come home to an empty house. And it was good she'd not forgotten about checking on Jaffa.

A Year 7 I didn't know very well came and asked if she could sit next to me, so I reluctantly moved my bag from the seat I was saving for Jazz and got a book out to read so that I wouldn't have to chat all the way home.

Bex was sitting at the kitchen table when I got in. She was flicking through a pet-supplies catalogue and sipping a mug of tea. She'd certainly made herself at home, I noted.

'Hi, Bertie!' She beamed her warm, cheery grin. 'How was school?'

'OK,' I said. I shrugged. 'Bit scary but I'll get over it,' I added hastily, seeing a concerned look cross Bex's face. 'Hey, where's Jaffs?' I scanned the room. I was pretty desperate to see my kitten and give her a cuddle.

'Aaaaaah. Little Jaffsie was curled up on the sofa in the sitting room last time I looked,' Bex said in a soppy voice, nodding towards the hall. 'Naughty thing's shattered, and I'm not surprised. It looked as if she'd had a house party with half the cats in the neighbourhood when I came in.'

'House party?' I asked, puzzled.

Bex was laughing. 'You should have seen the mess in here! Food everywhere, shredded bits of tissue paper . . . it looked like a younger version of Sparky had come to visit.'

'R-right,' I said shakily. That did not sound like my little cat at all. She had freaked out at being on her own all day, I knew it! 'So, er, how did Jaffa seem when you got in?' I tried to keep my voice light.

Bex stuck out her bottom lip. 'A bit nervy actually – but then I guess she felt guilty that she'd been caught in the act! It's OK, I've cleaned it all up now.'

'W-what act?' I stammered.

But before Bex could explain, a faint squeaking sound interrupted our conversation.

'Meeeeeee!'

I jumped. 'What was that?' I said.

Bex looked confused. 'What was what?'

I looked around the room carefully. 'Sounded like mewing, but it was kind of muffled. Are you sure Jaffa's in the sitting room?'

'Yes,' said Bex. 'I went in there to look for a pen to mark up this catalogue, and Jaffa was on the sofa. Then I came in here to make some tea.'

'Meeeeeeeeewwwww!'

'Listen!' I shouted. 'There it is again!'

Bex shook her head. 'Sorry, didn't hear a thing. Why don't you go and say hi to Jaffa?'

I ran into the sitting room, looking around wildly. No sign of Jaffa anywhere, just a small indentation on the sofa cushion where she liked to take a nap.

I whizzed back to Bex in the kitchen. 'She's not there now,' I said anxiously.

Bex was staring at the fridge with a bemused

expression on her face.

'I'm sure I heard a mew in here, you know,' I said, casting my eyes around the kitchen. 'Maybe she's stuck under the cupboards; she's done that before.' I was getting worried now.

'Jaffsie!' I called. 'Has something scared you? Where are you—?' I stopped when I realized Bex was looking at me strangely. 'What?' I asked nervously.

'Erm, well, I know this sounds odd, but I thought I heard a mew just now too, while you were in the sitting room . . .' she said haltingly, her eyes flicking back to the fridge. 'But – no, it couldn't have been.'

I gasped, one hand flying to my mouth. 'No! You don't think . . . ?' I rushed to the fridge and yanked the door open so brusquely the bottles and jars in the door clanked and wobbled dangerously.

There, on the middle shelf, her large light blue eyes peering out at me from between the yogurts

and the cheese, was my naughty little kitten.

'Me . . . is . . . f-f-f-f-reeeeeeezin'!' Her teeth were chattering!

'Oh, Jaffsie! What on earth possessed you to hide in the *fridge*?' I cried. 'How did you even get in there?' I reached in, cupped the poor shivering little kitten in my hands and held her close to me.

'Give her loads of cuddles!' Bex urged. 'Should I grab a blanket? Shall I call the ve—?'

'NO!' Jaffa jumped and I held her to me more firmly. 'No,' I repeated more calmly. 'Don't say the V-E-T word. She hates it,' I said, realizing how stupid that must sound. I didn't care though; I was more concerned about not upsetting Jaffa further after her ordeal. 'I'll just snuggle her and stroke her, and when she's warmed up a bit I'll give her a treat.'

Bex peered at Jaffa anxiously. 'OK, if you're sure. Maybe I should check on the Internet to see if there's any advice on caring for a freezing-cold cat?' she asked.

'Yes,' I said, my eyes lighting up. That would be a great way to get rid of her so I could actually talk to Jaffa in private. 'That would be kind of you,' I added, smiling in what I hoped was a grateful manner. I gently nuzzled Jaffa's gorgeous velvety fur. She had finally stopped quivering and was even starting to purr softly.

Bex nodded and hurried upstairs to the computer. I waited until she was out of earshot and then I lowered my voice and said, 'So are you going to tell me what's been going on?'

'Jaffsie a bit tired and sleepy now,' she whined, avoiding my gaze.

'Jaffa,' I warned, 'I think you should talk to me about this. Was it Bex? Did she shout at you – because of the mess she was telling me about?'

Jaffa jerked her chin up and shot me a wounded look. 'Me did NOT make mess!' she mewled.

I sighed. 'Bex told me that when she came in it looked as though her dog had been let loose in the house! So how are you going to explain that?'

Jaffa dropped her gaze and let out a snuffly noise that could have been her version of a sigh. 'If Bertie don't want to believe Jaffsie, then what can Jaffsie do?' she said pitifully.

I could see I was not going to get much sense out of her. Maybe she really *had* had a huge shock of some kind. Mind you, getting stuck in the fridge was enough of a shock in itself . . .

I went upstairs to Dad's study. Bex was tapping away at the computer keyboard and peering at the screen. She looked up when I coughed.

'Oh, hi! Sorry, got a bit sidetracked,' she said sheepishly. 'Happens whenever I look up anything about animals on the Internet!'

I grinned. 'Know what you mean,' I said,

pulling up a spare chair and plonking myself down beside her.

Bex was looking at a website called 'Curiosity Killed the Cat', which sounded a bit alarming, but as I scanned the page I was relieved to see that the real-life stories didn't contain anything more gruesome than cats who'd got stuck in trees, sheds, other people's garages, and so on. As it happened, there was one story of a cat who'd been shut in the fridge by mistake, and this had prompted a huge number of comments.

Cat-astrophic says: My cat, Badger, gave me the fright of my life this morning. I went to get some milk from the fridge, and when I opened the door Badger flew at me from the middle shelf! Goodness only knows how he got shut in there. Am gutted to think he slipped in without me noticing. Any tips on how to warm up a freezing moggie?

Kitty24 says: You must be a really stupid owner not to notice your cat had got into the fridge – didn't you see something moving when you went to shut the door?

Tomcat says: Actually, Kitty24, I think you'll find that cats are so swift and silent that it's quite easy for them to outwit their owners in this way.

Purrfect10 says: I agree with Tomcat. My cat, Mr Woo-woo, is always creeping up on us unawares and has been known to leap on to my head without warning, which can be quite upsetting.

Cats-Whiskers says: Take him to the vet, idiot. And talking of things idiotic, what is it with your cat's name????

Cat-astrophic says: @Tomcat and Purrfect10 – thanks! @Cats-Whiskers – Idiotic yourself. Take a look at Badger's photo.

'Badger's quite a cool name. I'd be pretty upset if I was called "Mr Woo-woo" though,' I sneered.

Bex laughed. 'People can sound crazy when it comes to their pets, can't they?'

I wondered if she thought *I* was crazy, espe-

cially since she'd heard me talking to Jaffa like she could understand every word I said. Which of course she could.

Bex carried on. 'But, hey, I'm a complete nut-case when it comes to Sparky! I love him to bits. If anything happened to upset him, I'd be right on to one of these chat rooms and I'd probably be writing five-page essays about it! Not that I can see Sparky finding it easy to hide behind the yogurts and the cheese – he'd probably scoff it all down in the blink of an eye and be left with nothing to hide behind. And I'd be left with a fridge full of freezing stuffed dog and nothing else!'

This conjured up such a bonkers image that I dissolved into fits of giggles, which then set Bex off too. Soon the pair of us were hooting and shrieking and coming up with even more loony ideas of what Sparky would get up to.

Perhaps having Bex around the place wasn't so bad after all.

5

Freaky Goings-On

'Good to see you two having fun.'

It was Dad. I'd been having such a blast with Bex that I hadn't heard him come in.

'Oh, hi!' I said, wiping tears of laughter from my face.

'Tee-hee! Er, hi,' said Bex coyly.

'Right . . . I-I'll just go and get on with my homework,' I stammered, pushing the chair back and making for the door. 'I've got shedloads of the stuff.'

'Oh no, you won't,' Dad said, barring the way. I looked up at him and realized that he was actually looking pretty grim-faced. 'You're not doing

anything or going anywhere until you've cleaned up the mess downstairs.'

'What?' Bex and I cried in unison.

Dad folded his arms and looked at us both, head on one side in a yeah-yeah-pull-the-other-one-why-don't-you expression. 'So you're telling me you have no idea how the kitchen got into the state I've just found it in?' he asked.

Bex and I looked at each other, jaws hanging open.

We followed him downstairs, Bex filling Dad in on what she had found when she'd come in from work earlier.

'Well, it looks like she's been up to even more tricks,' Dad said, as we walked into the kitchen, to be met by a pretty impressive replica of the scene Bex had described earlier.

'Oh my word, she *has* done it again!' Bex's voice rose in disbelief.

Jaffa was crouched on the worktop under an

open cupboard door, surrounded by what could only be described as a scene of devastation: ripped-up teabags, packets of crisps and peanuts, rice, pasta and cereals were tumbling off the surface on to the floor to join other shredded items of food and packaging, and yet more bits and pieces were falling out of the cupboard, as if Jaffa had, moments before, been rummaging about in there, throwing things over her shoulder in a frenzied hunt for something to eat.

'Jaffa!' I breathed.

'I have to say that whoever left the cupboard door open was a bit daft,' Dad said. I could tell he was trying to keep a lid on his temper for Bex's benefit.

'Well, it wasn't me,' said Bex, turning to me. 'And I know it wasn't Bertie because she was with me the whole time, weren't you?'

I nodded. 'That's right,' I said. 'Just had a cuddle with Jaffsie to warm her up and then we went

upstairs to Google something.'

'*Warm her up?*' Dad repeated incredulously. 'It's hardly the bleak midwinter out there.'

'No, er, I haven't had a chance to tell you that part,' said Bex anxiously. 'Jaffa got shut in the fridge.'

Dad's eyes bulged from his sockets and he let his hands fall to his sides. 'Whatever next?!' he exclaimed.

'Miiiiaaaaow!' Jaffa howled, backing into the wall, her forehead crumpled in fear, her hackles up along the back of her tiny neck. 'Bertie's dad not be cross with Jaffsie! Jaffsie not do it! Jaffsie frighted.'

'It's OK,' I said softly, making a move towards her.

'No, it's not OK!' said Dad firmly, stepping in front of me. 'She looks as guilty as sin, and so she should. You are not to go picking her up and cuddling her after what she's done or she'll think she can get away with it again!' Then he turned to Jaffa and shouted, 'You are a naughty girl!'

'Miiiiiaaaaaow! Me is NOT naughty! Tell him, Bertie,' Jaffa commanded. If she was a human I would have said she sounded tearful.

'Nigel,' said Bex in a measured tone of voice, 'she's only a kitten. It's probably just a phase—'

'I know she's only a kitten!' Dad cried in exasperation. 'That's what makes this so insane! If she can make this much mess when she's only a few months old, what on earth is it going to be like when she's older?'

Uh-oh. I heard alarm bells ringing urgently in the back of my mind.

'Oh, it's not that bad!' said Bex brightly. 'I'll have this lot cleared up in no time. Bertie – why don't you stick the kettle on? Your dad looks a bit frazzled.'

Even though I was thankful that Bex was

speaking up for my little cat, I nevertheless couldn't silence a nagging doubt: what if Jaffa was behaving in this bizarre way because she didn't like 'the Bexy lady' that much after all? What if this was her way of showing me just how much she hated my leaving her alone all day?

Dad sat down heavily, put his head in his hands and groaned quietly. 'I always thought having a pet would be hard work, but I never thought little Jaffsie was capable of creating such a disaster area. I mean, look at her!'

Jaffsie had made herself as small as possible and was shivering as she surveyed us with unblinking sapphire-blue eyes. 'Me really is sorry, Bertie. Really me is,' she whispered. 'But you gotta believe it's not Jaffsie's fault.'

I just stood by the kettle, shaking my head, not knowing what to say to anyone.

Bex came back in with a mop and a dustpan and brush. 'Kettle on?' she chirruped.

I gave a brief nod.

'Great. Take these, Bertie,' she said, handing me the dustpan and brush. 'You sweep and I'll mop.'

'Bex, you shouldn't be doing that!' Dad protested.

'Nonsense, you've only just got in. Relax,' said Bex. 'Jaffa *will* grow out of this, I'm sure.'

'Me is not growin' out of nothin'!' Jaffa protested. 'Cos me has not grown *into* nothin' in the first place!'

'I know,' I said in as soothing a voice as I could manage.

'Well, I don't!' said Dad irritably. 'This behaviour is freaky, if you ask me.'

I sniggered in spite of myself. Dad always sounds weird when he uses words like 'freaky', as though he's trying to sound younger than he is.

He shot me an angry look, so I bent down and began sweeping furiously.

'No, really,' said Bex, beaming at Dad. 'Jaffa's

growing up and she's approaching adolescence in cat years, so it's not that strange to see her flexing her muscles a bit, putting her stamp on things.'

'What is the lady sayin' with all those big words?' Jaffa asked.

'You're growing up and it won't be long before you're a teenager!' I said as quietly as I could.

'What's that? A teenager?' Dad snapped distractedly. 'That's all I need. It's bad enough having a hormonal daughter without having to look after a moody cat as well.'

'Thanks a lot!' I cried.

'No, no, it's not as bad as all that,' Bex said hurriedly. 'It's like I said: Jaffa's probably just going through a bit of a phase. But she'll settle down quickly enough, you'll see.'

'Mmm.' Dad was not going to be convinced that easily. 'But you don't seriously think that she could have opened the cupboard on her own, do you? Are you sure neither of you left it ajar, even a tiny bit, by mistake? And what about her getting into the fridge? How did that happen?'

Bex stopped mopping and she and I exchanged puzzled glances. 'I've no idea,' she said. She sounded as though she was getting a bit peeved with Dad now. For some reason that made me feel bad. I didn't want them to argue. 'I was sitting at the table when Bertie came in, looking through some pet-supplies catalogues, and Bertie didn't even have time to make herself a drink because we heard this mewing coming from the fridge and – well, we ended up looking stuff up on the Internet about cats getting stuck in weird places. Which is when you came in . . .' She tailed off.

'So cats can open cupboards and fridges?' Dad said sceptically.

I found myself thinking that if this was true, my little kitten would have to be freakishly strong.

'Looks like we're going to have plenty of fun and games on our hands while Jaffa goes through

this "phase" of hers, doesn't it?' Dad added.

'You could fix safety locks on the cupboards,' Bex suggested. 'You know, like people do for small children. I think you can get them for the fridge as well.'

Dad went to the kettle, which had just boiled, and poured water into the mugs I'd set out. 'Not a bad idea,' he said. 'Still, it's a lot of effort to go to and I'm not the world's greatest DIY expert.'

You can say that again, I thought. I remembered the day he'd promised to fix some shelves for me and had decided it would save time if he didn't remove the contents first. Everything had come tumbling down on top of him and he'd broken his glasses, my animal ornaments and his nose. I was pretty miffed about the ornaments. I'd spent years collecting them.

I swept up the last of the mess into the pan and chucked it in the bin just as Bex said to Dad, 'Let's go and have another look on the Internet. I can show you the stuff I found about cats who get stuck in daft places and maybe we can search for some ways to prevent it happening again.'

'I've got a better idea,' said Dad. 'Why don't I phone for a curry and we all crash out in front of a DVD once Bertie's finished her homework? I'm bushed.'

Jaffa was pretty happy to join us that evening. I felt a bit odd though, squashed up next to Dad and Bex on the sofa. I kept wondering if they would have preferred it if I hadn't been there. But I couldn't exactly ask them that. I sighed inwardly. At least I didn't have to worry about Jaffa while she was safely with us; she was not likely to get herself shut in the fridge again after getting so cold.

The only 'chilling' she would be doing for the rest of the evening would be with us in front of the telly.

6

Another Mystery Mess

The next morning I was woken by Dad crashing into my room, his hair sticking up like an electrocuted porcupine and his expression fierce.

'Get up at once, young lady!' he commanded, charging over to the curtains and wrenching them open.

'W-what time is it?' I asked blurrily. I propped myself up on one elbow and blinked at the watery September sunlight which was shining directly on to my face. I felt like a mole coming blindly out of its tunnel, and frankly I wished I could burrow right back down again into the snuggly dark warmth of my duvet.

'Six o'clock!' Dad barked, storming over to the door. He stood there, hands on hips, glaring at me.

'Six . . . ? But that's the middle of the *night*!' I whined, pulling my duvet up and preparing to wriggle back underneath it.

Dad was too quick for me; he yanked hold of the edge and swiftly tugged it off me, saying, 'My sentiments exactly, but sadly you have a kitten who does not seem to know the difference between night and day.'

I closed my eyes and shook my head, hoping in vain that this was a nightmare that would soon go away. I looked up. No good. Dad was still there.

I swung my legs over the side of the bed and staggered across the room to find my slippers. 'What's she done now?' I asked warily, running my fingers through my out-of-control curls.

'Words fail me,' Dad said sharply. 'You had better come and see for yourself.'

Something in Dad's tone had the effect of flick-

ing a switch on inside my brain. I careered down to the kitchen as fast as my sleep-heavy legs would carry me and saw . . . well, at first I wasn't sure what I saw. The kitchen was in the kind of state you might expect to find if a bomb had exploded in the middle of it. Chairs were knocked on their sides, a couple of mugs lay broken on the floor, a trail of cat biscuits formed a path from the utility room, and J-cloths and tea towels lay scattered all over the place, cupboard doors were open . . . and Jaffa was sitting on top of one of the highest of those cupboards, shaking and mewing pitifully.

'Jaffa,' I said sadly, 'how could you?'

'But Jaffsie didn't do it!' she whinged. 'Jaffsie's a good girl—'

'Jaffa, if you didn't do this—'

'Of course she did this!' Dad had caught up with me and was standing behind me, surveying the scene of devastation with a look of utter distaste. 'I'm sorry, Bertie, but you're going to have to shut her in the utility room while you're at school today. I will clear all the surfaces in there before I go out so she can't knock anything over. I've got another meeting so I'll have to ask Bex if she can come round again.'

I started to protest. 'Jaffa only started behaving like this when she was left on her own!'

'Bertie,' said Dad firmly, 'I can't let Jaffa have the run of the house if she's going to behave like this while we're out. I don't care if it's a "phase". Either you accept my terms and conditions, or . . .' He tailed off and fixed me with a rather menacing stare.

He was threatening my little cat with eviction!

'But, Dad,' I started. I tried hard to sound reasonable despite the wobble in my voice.

'*But nothing*, young lady,' Dad snapped. 'I am very fond of Jaffa, you know that, but I can't have this.' His voice had such a note of finality to it that

I knew there was no point in arguing.

'I'm going to get dressed,' he said.

'I'll clear this up. It will be as if nothing ever happened,' I promised frantically.

I waited until Dad had gone upstairs. My first priority was to talk to my kitten, who was gazing at me with the most innocent-looking flashing blue eyes, a worried frown creasing her fluffy orange face. I couldn't help thinking that she did not look to me like a cat who felt at all guilty. Terrified, more like.

I carefully picked up one of the chairs and carried it over to the cupboard, then climbed on to it and reached to get Jaffa down.

'Jaffsie not naughty!' she mewled. 'Nasty big—oh!' She stopped herself.

'What, Jaffa?' She had been about to tell me something important, I was sure of it. I carefully placed one hand under her soft tummy and whispered encouragingly, 'Nasty big what?'

Jaffa seemed to shake her head. She let me pick her up, but her ears were flat and her needle-sharp claws clung to my flesh, making me wince slightly. 'Me can't say,' she said finally. Her small voice was quaking.

'Jaffsie,' I said slowly, holding her away from me so that I could look her directly in the eye, 'are you keeping a secret from me?'

Jaffa dug her claws more deeply into my hand and blinked. 'N-nooo,' she said quietly.

'Jaffsie?' I said disbelievingly.

'NO!' she squeaked, suddenly wriggling hard. Then she did something she had never done before. She nipped me hard on the finger, her teeth bared in fury.

'Yeeee-ouch!' I yelled, staggering back and letting Jaffa leap free from my clutches. She hared out of the kitchen and bolted through to the sitting room.

I sat down heavily on the kitchen chair I had

just been standing on and rubbed my hand, tears springing to my eyes. What was happening to my little cat?

I was still raking over the morning's events when I ran to catch the bus to school. Why had Jaffa bitten me? Why wouldn't she talk to me? Why was she being so – well – *mean*? It wasn't my fault I had to go to school.

I fought my way down the aisle, stepping over legs sticking out as if placed there on purpose to trip me up, and trying to avoid thwacking people with my bag. My head was way up in the clouds, so I didn't notice who I'd plonked myself down next to until he prodded me on the shoulder and said:

'Hey, not speaking to me?'

I turned, frowning, and saw who it was. 'Oh, hey, it's you!' I said. I immediately flushed pink at how stupid that must have sounded.

Fergus grinned and flicked his floppy dark

red fringe out of his eyes. 'Too busy taking people out with your kamikaze rucksack to notice your mates?' he teased.

I smiled in relief. He didn't think I was stupid.

'So, how'd it go yesterday?' he asked.

'Oh, well, she's acting odd. I knew she wouldn't adapt well to this whole school thing,' I mumbled distractedly. I fiddled with my hair in an attempt to make it stay tied back in the gross yellow scrunchie, which had been the only one to hand as I was running out of the door. Corkscrew curls were doing their usual escapologist trick and sticking to my hot and sweaty face. 'Not a good look,' as Jazz would say.

'She always acts odd, doesn't she?' Fergus said jokily. 'I thought she was her usual hyper self when I saw her. Haven't seen her this morning yet – have you? Maybe she got a lift in.'

I was jolted out of my dreamy state, puzzled by what Fergus had just said. 'Who're you talking about?'

Fergus laughed. 'Who d'you think?'

I stared at him blankly.

He raised his eyebrows 'Wow, are you dopey today! Something's up, isn't it?'

I started again to tell him about Jaffa, but I thought better of it when I noticed a group of the Year 9 girls from the day before – Kezia and her friends – making their way towards us. They were looking at Fergus and me, then giggling to one another as they lurched and tripped their way down the aisle. I had a nasty feeling about those girls and I didn't want them hearing me talking to Fergus about my kitten.

'No, no,' I said quickly. 'Nothing's bothering me, honest. So, what about you? How're you feeling? About school, I mean.' Lame topic of conversation, but I had to say something.

Fergus shrugged and pulled a face. 'School's just school,' he said. 'I've moved around so much, I reckon it doesn't really matter where I go, as long as I've got my music, that is. The teachers are all pains, there's always a bunch of boys who only want to play football and punch each other, and there's always a bunch of girls who only want to paint their nails and whisper and giggle.'

He looked pointedly at the three miniskirted girls gossiping and shrieking their way past us.

I let out a snort of laughter. Too right.

'But there's one thing I've never had before at any of the other schools I've been to,' Fergus said, suddenly more serious. He stared at me for a bit longer than was comfortable.

'Oh yeah – what's that?' I muttered, looking away. The straps on my rucksack had just become incredibly interesting.

'I've never had a friend who's a girl before,' he said quietly. I looked up sharply in spite of myself. 'It's cool,' he added.

Get a grip, Bertie! I told myself. He's only being nice to you cos he doesn't have any other

friends yet. I looked around quickly to see where Kezia and her mates were, but they were out of earshot, thank goodness.

There was an awkward silence as I couldn't think of anything to say.

'So,' Fergus said lightly. 'How's Jaffa?'

'Well, that's what I was trying to say earlier,' I said, grateful for the change of subject. 'She's acting in a freaky way. I was going to ask your advice, seeing as you probably know more about cats than I do.'

'Oh, right! I thought you were talking about Jazz. No wonder you looked at me weirdly!' he laughed.

'Yeah, no wonder!' I laughed too. I found myself looking around, wondering vaguely where Jazz was. Maybe I should see if she'd texted me.

Fergus nudged me. 'Go on then, tell me what's up.'

So I launched into a description of the chaos

my kitten had caused, and was just getting to the part where Jaffa had got herself shut in the fridge when I was aware of someone leaning right over me.

I looked up slowly to see Kezia, or rather her unfeasibly long legs, pressing against the side of my seat.

'You see Rashid yesterday?' she was saying to Fergus.

I gawped at her. Could she not *see* me? Was I, like, totally *invisible*, or did she think I was too small to be bothered with? She was crushing me, forcing me back into my seat so that she could lean over and talk to Fergus.

Fergus's face flushed. He looked up from under his fringe and said, 'Oh, hey, Kez. I – er, yeah, I spoke to him. He says it's cool, I'm in. You were right – they did need a drummer. We're going to meet again tonight. Thanks for putting a word in.'

So I *was* invisible, and not just to the girl.

Fergus and I had been having a conversation, but now he was acting like I wasn't there. It was horrible. I couldn't even escape, because 'Kez' was blocking my way with her monstrously long legs. I wriggled around a bit and had just about managed to get slightly more comfortable when something horrible happened.

My rucksack began to move – of its own accord.

7

Stowaway

At first I tried telling myself it was only the bus that was causing the movement, because it did make everything jolt when it stopped and started in the heavy rush-hour traffic. But there was no mistaking it, the bumping and jogging was actually going on *right inside my bag*. It felt as though there was something in there, trying to get out. Maybe it was my mobile – I might have set it to vibrate by mistake.

The bag lurched again. That was no mobile! It would have to have been set to 'mega-turbo-vibrate' to move around that much.

A horrible thought occurred to me. Oh no!

What if Jaffa had brought me a 'present'? Kaboodle, her uncle, used to do that. He once left a mouse in my shoe when I was looking after him during my pet-sitting days, and Dad had found other 'gifts' from Kaboodle in all kinds of inappropriate places. What if Jaffa was feeling guilty about nipping me and had tried to make amends by leaving a mouse in my school bag? I had heard stories of mice playing dead, the cat thinking they had finished off their prey, only for the rodent to come to life the minute the cat had gone away.

I glanced up to see if Fergus or Kezia had noticed, but they were too busy jabbering about the band.

Rustle. Rustle.

There it was again! And this time the movement was accompanied by a distinctly squeaky noise.

I shoved my fist in my mouth to stop myself from screaming. My heart was fluttering like a trapped butterfly, but there was no way I was going to lose the plot in front of Fergus and that girl.

'Excuse me,' I said firmly. I pushed myself up to standing so that Kezia had to stop leaning over me and let me out into the aisle.

Even then she didn't look at me properly, just curled her lip in a sour impression of a smile and slid into my empty seat so she could lean in to Fergus even closer. I was focusing on keeping a hold on my jumping, squeaking bag. But even as I wriggled past people's rucksacks and legs and prayed that I would not make a fool of myself in front of the whole bus by tripping over and falling on my face, I saw Fergus roll his eyes and shoot me a sheepish lopsided grin over the top of Kezia's head.

I didn't have time to think what that meant; I had to get to the front of the bus so that when it stopped I could be the first to get off. I would have to run and dump the mouse round the corner from the school gate so that it didn't come into the yard with me.

I shuddered and willed the bus to get to school faster: my mind was full of images of a monster mouse with savage teeth, making a meal out of the books in my bag.

At last the bus pulled up outside the gates. It was as if an invisible hand had turned up the volume: the giggling and gossiping from everyone on board increased as they scrambled to their feet and collected their belongings. I muttered a quick 'thank you' to the driver as he opened the doors to let me off, and then I legged it.

'Hey, wait up, Bertie!' I could hear Jazz calling me, but didn't stop. Even though part of me badly wanted some help with whatever it was in my bag, I somehow didn't think my best mate would be much use faced with a mouse. She was the kind of girl who screamed if a ladybird landed on her hand.

I gritted my teeth and pounded the pavement, putting as much distance as I could between myself and the other kids. Then, once I was sure I was out of sight, I opened my bag.

'Bertie is not being careful today!' A small voice that I recognized only too well bleated at me from the depths of my rucksack.

I peered into the dark interior in astonishment. '*Jaffa?*' I said. It couldn't be. My mind really was playing tricks on me now.

'Course me's Jaffa,' said an irritable voice. 'Who does you think me is?' And with that, a little ginger-and-white face appeared, looking very cross indeed. My kitten bared her tiny sharp teeth and hissed. 'Me is not liking all the bumpy-bumpy. What is you doing to Jaffsie today? Me is only wanting a little snooze time.'

'J-Jaffa!' I stammered. 'What are you doing in my bag?'

'Me's just tellin' you. Is you stupid or something? Me is havin' a snooze time. Or me was, before all the bumpy-bumpy—'

'OK!' I cut in frantically. 'Listen, you may've thought you were just having a "snooze", but as it happens you were "snoozing" in my school bag, and now we're at school and I have to go in for register and I don't have the faintest idea what I'm going to do with you!'

'Bertie?'

I whirled round, my free hand clamped to my mouth. Fergus was standing a couple of metres away, looking concerned.

'Are you OK? You don't look too good. Do you feel sick?'

I glanced down and saw with relief that Jaffa had ducked into the bag, out of sight.

'Yes, no, I mean, I'm fine,' I babbled, grinning

like the Cheshire Cat with a bucket of cream. 'I think I've dropped something, that's all. You go in – the bell's about to ring.'

Fergus looked dubious. 'I don't think you look fine at all. You were leaning over with your head in your bag like you were about to throw up. And you've gone white! Let me take you to the sick room. We can call your dad.'

'No!' I almost shouted. 'No,' I repeated, more softly. 'Honestly, I'm fine. I just thought I'd forgotten my science book, that's all—'

'I thought you said you'd dropped something,' Fergus interrupted suspiciously.

'Yes!' I said brightly. 'I dropped my pencil and then, when I bent down to pick it up and put it in my bag, I thought, Oh no! I've forgotten my science book!'

What a numpty! I should tell him the truth . . .

'Ferrr-guuus!' Kezia was calling him from the school gates. 'Are you coming or what?'

I realized with a sinking heart that I couldn't tell him about Jaffa. Not with Kezia there. She would think I was a right baby. Either that or completely insane. I was going to have to deal with this little problem alone.

The bell was ringing shrilly, cutting through the crisp early-autumn air.

'Go,' I said, raising my eyebrows and flicking my head in Kezia's direction.

Fergus looked torn for an instant, then his face crumpled and he shot me a look of annoyance mixed with something like despair.

My stomach tied itself into a tight knot as I wished he would ignore the other girl and come over. Then he would see Jaffa and realize what an awful predicament I was in. But then I found myself wanting him to go off with that girl and to stop feeling sorry for me. My confusion exploded into anger.

I'm not some little puppy who needs looking

after, I thought bitterly as I watched him turn and run through the gates.

'Has the Fergus gone?' Jaffa mewed from inside the bag.

'Yes,' I growled. 'No thanks to you. Now listen to me, Jaffa. You have already got me into big trouble at home – AND you hurt me this morning! I am *not* going to get into trouble at school as well because of you. Argh! I don't know what to do! I can't take you home because I have to go to my form room now, and I can't call Dad because he's out at a meeting, so I guess you know what this means.'

'Yes,' said Jaffa solemnly, blinking at me from among the jumble of books and stationery. 'Jaffsie will sit with Bertie and be a good girl aaaaall day.'

I felt totally knotted up with exasperation at this silly little kitten. The idea of her sitting calmly on my desk as if it was the most normal thing in the world while our form tutor, Mr Boyd, took the

register, was quite ridiculous.

'No, Jaffsie,' I said firmly, drawing down the flap of my rucksack to cover her up. 'You're going to snuggle down and have a lovely long snooze just like you'd planned to, while I work hard at my lessons. And I am not going to hear a *peep* out of you until we are safely back at home at the end of the day. Understood?'

Jaffsie yawned extravagantly and nodded as I covered her up. 'Me is feeling just a teensy-weensy bit sleepyhead anyway,' she said. 'Me will just be as quiet as a tiny baby mouse who is very *veee-rrry* quiet. You'll see.'

8
Gruesome Twosome

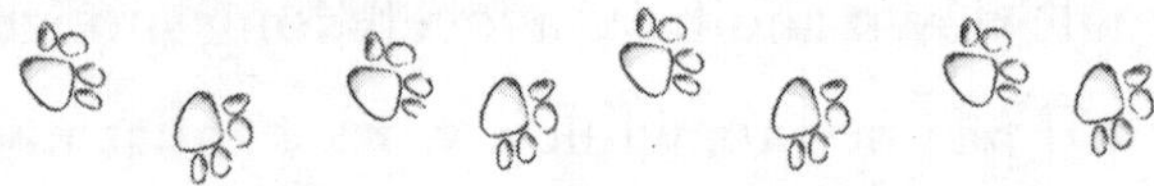

It was possibly the worst day of my life. I just about got away with Jaffa's snoring (which, by the way, was amazingly loud for such a small cat) by saying it was my stomach rumbling. And I think I convinced our maths teacher, Mrs Small, that the squeaking she found so aggravating was my chair, and I promised not to swing on it again. Every time a teacher's back was turned, or there was enough classroom noise for me to hide behind, I would bend down and hiss for Jaffa to keep quiet.

To her credit, Jaffa did at least refrain from trying to talk to me, but I was so nervy anyway that it didn't make much difference. I spent the whole

morning avoiding people and walking around with my rucksack glued to me. It was so stressful that, come lunchtime, I decided I could not go through the rest of the day like that, so I went to ask permission to call Bex. I would have to ask her to come and get Jaffa.

Luckily the secretary didn't ask any awkward questions, and she went to the other side of the office to do some photocopying while I made the call. Nevertheless, I felt excruciatingly guilty about all the deception and made an effort to kept my voice low.

'Hi, Bex. It's me, Bertie.'

'Bertie? Why are you calling? Is everything all right?' Bex said nervously.

'Yes, well, not really. Listen, can you come to school in the next half-hour? It's a bit of an emergency, but it's OK, I'm not hurt or anything. I just – I just couldn't think of anyone else to call, what with Dad in a meeting and everything,' I said, flustered. The secretary was coming back over.

'Erm, OK, yes. Shouldn't be a problem. Ruth's in again today, she can cover. But listen, I was just about to go and check on Jaffa – do you want me to—'

'That's just it,' I said quickly. 'It's because of her that I need you here right now! I – I can't explain on the phone.' The secretary was looking at me inquisitively.

I put on a bright, cheerful voice and said, 'That would be sooo kind of you, Bex. You know where the school is, don't you? That's right! I'll meet you in the reception area.'

'Bertie?' said Bex.

I didn't give her a chance to ask any more questions; I turned the phone off and left the office, praying she would come quickly.

Just my luck: Jazz spotted me in the corridor and came running over. She and I had not been in the same lessons that morning as we were in differ-

ent maths and English sets. Normally I would have been over the moon to hook up with her and go into lunch together, but this was not good timing. I pretended I hadn't seen her and ducked into the girls' loos, clutching my rucksack, which ominously was starting to wriggle again.

I had my hand on the door when I felt someone clutch the back of my jumper.

'Hey, slow down, Bert!' Jazz panted. 'You avoiding me?' she asked, her chocolate-drop eyes locking with mine. 'I tried saying hi this morning, but you were, like, totally manic, pushing your way off the bus and then running away. What've I done?'

I hugged my bag close to my chest and said in a panicky voice, 'Nothing, nothing! I'm just desperate for the loo.'

'Oh, right,' said Jazz, eyeing my bag suspiciously. 'Hey, listen – you haven't got my mobile, have you?' she added.

'No, of course not!' I said irritably.

'OK, OK. Chillax, girl!' Jazz flapped her hands at me. 'I just wondered. I mean, I've lost it and I just thought my *best mate* might be interested. Seeing as how we text each other all the time and everything. Or maybe you hadn't even *noticed* that I haven't been texting you.'

'Jazz,' I said shortly. 'I'm sorry about your phone. I did think it was odd you hadn't texted,' I fibbed – I hadn't even checked, what with everything that had been going on.' But I do kind of need the loo quite badly right this minute. I'll help you look for the phone later, OK?'

'Whatever,' Jazz said crossly. 'I'll see you in the lunch queue – save you a place?'

I nodded, hardly daring to breathe. She gave my bag one last glance and then headed in the direction of the lunch hall.

I let out the breath I'd been holding. As soon as the coast was clear, I nipped over to reception and was relieved to see Bex's little red car pulling up

outside the school gates. It was a good job her shop was not too far away. I stood right by the door so that I could talk to her without anyone hearing.

She spotted me immediately and came running over, her features etched with concern.

'Bertie! You look very pale. Are you sure you're all right? Your voice was so faint on the phone—'

I thrust the rucksack into her arms and said, 'She's in there, Bex! I think she's sleeping now. She totally freaked me out! She came to *school* with me! It's been a nightmare. You've got to take her home.'

'Slow down!' Bex said, putting the bag on the ground before grabbing hold of my shoulders firmly. 'What on earth is going on?'

'Bex,' I said, taking a deep breath, 'I don't know how this happened, and it's definitely not my fault, but Jaffa must have climbed into my bag this morning, and I didn't realize until I got to school. Please will you take her home for me?'

I gulped, all the stress of the morning finally overwhelming me.

'Oh my . . .!' Bex snatched up my bag and peered carefully in through the flap.

Jaffa let out an anguished mew. 'Miiiiiiaaaaaooooow! It dark and nasty in here! Me wanna go hoooome!'

'Oh dear, that naughty little kitten is giving you a hell of a time, isn't she?' Bex breathed. Her forehead creased in a frown. 'First the fridge, now your bag; anyone would think she was trying to hide from something! I'll take her right away. Don't you *need* your bag?'

'No, just take it!' I said. 'I'm sorry Bex, but I've got to go. Will you stay at home and wait for me if Dad doesn't get back before me?'

Bex put a hand on my shoulder and smiled warmly. 'Of course I will. You're not to worry about a thing. See you later.'

She waved as she went to her car.

I shot a furtive glance at the school office as I made my way into lunch, but thankfully the secretary was involved in a heated argument with one of the sixth-formers, so she didn't notice me.

I made it into lunch in time to be given the dregs of the pasta Bolognese just as Jazz was getting up from the table with her tray. She had eaten without me.

'Thanks for waiting, Jazz,' I said sarcastically, coming over.

'Thanks for not turning up,' she said, flicking her head back and setting her beads off in an irritated rattle.

'I just did!' I protested. 'Oh please, don't be like that, Jazz. I've had a terrible morning—'

'Tell me about it!' Jazz said, plonking herself back into her seat and setting her tray down with a bang. 'How am I supposed to function without my phone? This "handing in" business was bad enough, but now it's just *disappeared*!'

I chewed the inside of my mouth as Jazz prattled on. She was always losing stuff. She'd probably left it somewhere at home. I tuned back in to her ranting, which had moved on from phones now.

'And what *is* it with all this homework they're giving us? Mr Greg gave us a ton of English to be handed in, like, *tomorrow*. I just can't get my head around it. And it's *so* unfair cos it means I have even less time to practise for my street-dance class – which is, like, totally *immense*, by the way. The teacher is awesome. And I *so* wanted to take up singing lessons, cos Kezia is like, "The singing teacher here is way cool," but Mum's just like, "No *way* are you taking on something else right now, young lady," and I just . . .'

Hmm. What was so fantastic about this Kezia? She had her claws into Fergus, and Jazz seemed totally smitten with her too.

I let Jazz wibble on while I munched the cold pasta and thought about Jaffa's stowaway antics.

What on earth had possessed her? I didn't buy that rubbish about wanting some 'snooze time'.

'Bertie? Hell-loooo!' Jazz was waving her hands in front of my face. 'Is there any life on Planet Bertie? Do we need to send out a search party?'

I raised my eyebrows. 'Very funny.'

'Well, ex-cuuuse me,' said Jazz, hands on hips, 'but if I didn't know you better, I'd say you haven't been listening to a word I've been saying! You look like you're on Planet Zombie.'

'It was Planet Bertie a minute ago,' I said wearily.

'Whatever,' said Jazz. She had her you-are-*so*-not-going-to-get-away-with-this look on her face, the one where she fixes me intently with her dark brown eyes and sets her mouth in a grim expression.

I rolled my eyes.

'Hey, *Jasmeena*,' said a sneery voice.

Jazz whirled round, her back to me as she looked up at the speaker. She flushed with pleasure when she saw who it was. 'Hey, Kezia!'

The older girl stood with a hand on one hip, her mouth set in a sly smirk. She was accompanied by one of her creepy mates – Charlie, Fergus had said her name was. The pair of them looked like they were trying to model themselves on some kind of girl band. They wore mega-short skirts, enough make-up to sink a ship, and their hair was slicked back into high ponytails and held in place with shiny hairclips. They also wore gross huge hooped earrings, which hung below their jawline. They chewed gum as they spoke, their eyes hard, their expressions somehow managing to look disdainful even when they smiled. A right Gruesome Twosome.

Has Halloween come early? I wondered.

'Charlie and I thought you might want a look at this, seeing as how you're so, like, *famous* and

everything,' Kezia said, shoving a piece of paper under Jazz's nose.

Jazz's eyes sparkled as she read what was on it, and I watched her expression turn to one of total joy. I looked over her shoulder and saw the words:

screaming out in bold red-and-black writing. A sick feeling churned in my stomach.

'Can. You. Believe it?' Jazz breathed, her hands flying to her face in ecstasy. 'This is soooo mega. It'll be just like *Who's Got Talent?* Oh, Bertie. Isn't this cool?' She read out the words on the poster:

CAN YOU SING? CAN YOU DANCE?
HAVE YOU ALWAYS DREAMED
OF BEING A STAR?
THEN THIS COULD BE YOUR CHANCE!

'TALENT' NEEDED FOR
THE SCHOOL SHOW...

COME TO THE HALL AFTER
SCHOOL ON FRIDAY AND SHOW US
WHAT YOU'RE MADE OF!

'Yeah, we thought you'd be up for it, *Jasmeena*.'

I winced at their use of Jazz's full name. She normally hated it when people called her that. But instead of correcting the girls sharply as she would

usually have done, she simply gushed, 'Wow, this is, like, awesome!'

'Yeah,' said Kezia. She twirled her shiny dark ponytail with one long painted fingernail and gave Jazz a tight-lipped smile. 'I'm sure you'll have loads to teach us *amateurs*. Won't you, babe?'

'After all,' added Charlie in a sugary voice, 'you are *best mates* with Danni Minnow, aren't you? She must have given you loads of top tips on how to make it as a performer.'

'Yeah,' said Kezia. 'I mean, no one else will have that kind of an advantage, will they?'

The two girls exchanged knowing looks and burst into giggles. 'Oh, Jazzie,' Charlie said casually, and the pair turned to go, 'did you drop this?' She dangled a phone carelessly from her fingertips.

'Hey, my phone!' Jazz gasped, her jaw falling to the floor. 'Wow, where did you find it?'

'Nowhere,' Charlie said, a bit too quickly. 'Like I said, you probably dropped it.'

Jazz's forehead creased and she opened her mouth to say something.

'Come on, Charlie,' Kezia said impatiently. 'Can't stand around here all day. Catch you later, girls,' she cooed back at us over her shoulder.

Jazz shook her head in disbelief and then shot me a face-splitting grin. 'Aren't they, like, *awesome*?' she swooned.

I was saved from having to comment by the sound of the bell for afternoon lessons.

9

A Canine Plan

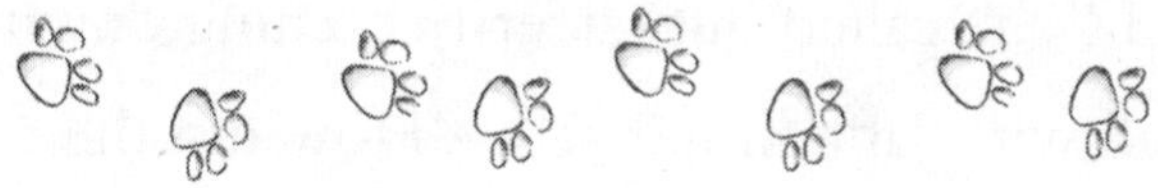

I couldn't wait to get home. Jazz had spent the whole bus journey holding court to anyone who would listen about how she and Danni Minnow were such close mates and how she was going to email her that night about Kezia's auditions. I looked out in vain for Fergus until I remembered that he had been at another band rehearsal.

I let myself into the house to find Bex waiting for me, as she had promised. It felt good to see her smiling face – so good, in fact, that it occurred to me I must have been crazy ever to think I didn't want Dad getting to know her. If he was going

to have anyone as a girlfriend, I was beginning to realize I was glad it was someone as warm-hearted and kind as Bex.

'Hi!' she called out cheerily, coming down into the hall with Jaffa in her arms. 'How did the rest of your day go?'

'Much better, thanks,' I said. 'How's little Jaffsie?'

'Jaffsie is very happy with the lovely Bexy lady,' my cat purred, yawning and shaking her ears.

Bex laughed. 'Anyone would think you two understood each other!' she joked.

I bit my lips to stop myself from laughing too. If only she knew!

'Hungry? I made some biscuits this after-noon – didn't really know what to do with myself while I was waiting for you.'

'You can come here any time!' I said, following her into the kitchen, where the aroma of baking filled my nostrils.

As I tucked into some delicious chocolate-chip biscuits Bex sat opposite me with Jaffa curled up, fast asleep, on her lap.

'You might think I'm crazy suggesting this,' she said, 'but, you know I said it was almost as if Jaffa was hiding from something?'

I nodded, my mouth full of crumbs.

'Well, I've been thinking, and, I suppose it's a long shot, but . . . maybe that's *exactly* what she's been doing. Maybe something has been getting into the house and terrorizing her – and causing all the chaos,' she added.

I must have looked alarmed because Bex reached over the table to put a hand on my arm and said gently, 'Don't worry, it's not that I've seen anything . . . but the thing is, with a cat flap . . . well, put it this way, if Jaffa can get in and out, other animals could as well, couldn't they?'

I swallowed the mouthful of biscuit and said, 'Another cat, you mean?'

'That would be the obvious answer, yes,' said Bex. 'Although I wonder if Jaffa would be so scared by another cat . . .'

A worrying thought was forming in my mind. 'Oh no! You don't reckon a dog could get in, do you?'

Bex pulled down the corners of her mouth and reflected for a moment. 'No. No, I don't think that's likely,' she said finally. 'I mean, a large dog such as a Labrador or a collie – or a Springer spaniel, come to that – wouldn't be able to fit. They'd get their head in and that would be that.' She sniggered at the idea. 'And if you're thinking of smaller breeds, such as a Jack Russell, a chihuahua or even a Border like Sparky, well, I just can't see it happening,' she went on. 'For a start, where would it come from? Even if a dog was a stray, it would have to find its way into your back garden somehow, which would be tricky, seeing as the side gate's always shut.'

I nodded. That made sense. Plus I didn't actu-

ally know a whole lot of people in our area with dogs. There was only Mr Bruce with his two King Charles spaniels, but they were either kept indoors or on a leash because they were so bouncy. I couldn't see Mr Bruce letting his 'two boys', as he called them, out of his sight for an instant.

I wished Jaffa would simply be honest with me and tell me what was going on, I thought miserably.

'Wait a minute!' said Bex, cutting into my gloomy thoughts. 'All this talk about dogs has given me an idea. Now, I don't know how your dad would feel about this . . . but what if I could persuade him to let Sparky come over with me on Friday night?'

'Er . . . yeah. I guess,' I said, frowning. I wasn't sure how Sparky was going to help. And Jaffa was already scared enough as it was.

'I was thinking,' Bex said, 'Sparky's a pretty brave little pooch. Borders are feisty hunters, you know. They're bred to go down holes and ferret out – er, well, ferrets! And rabbits and rats. That kind of thing.'

I stared at her, rather alarmed at the turn this conversation was taking.

Bex laughed. 'Don't look at me like that! I'm thinking of using Sparky to *protect* Jaffa, not frighten her any more than she is already!' she said. 'Listen, you reckon Jaffa's not to blame for everything that's been happening, right? But you haven't got any proof either way, and it looks like it's going to be pretty tricky to *get* proof, as the intruder seems to be crafty enough to know it can only come in while no humans are around.'

'Right,' I said.

'Soooo,' said Bex slowly, as if incredulous that I had not yet got the point, 'Sparky could be shut in the utility room, near the cat flap, while we keep Jaffa safely out of the way. If the animal decides to chance its luck again, it will have Sparky to reckon with!'

Bex sounded a lot more positive than I felt about this idea, but I had to admit I hadn't come up with anything better.

'OK,' I said. 'Sounds like a plan.'

Dad agreed right away that Sparky could come over that Friday night. I was a bit gobsmacked by what was happening to Dad lately, to be honest.

'First he goes and falls head over heels for you and lets me keep you,' I said to Jaffa, 'then he gets himself a girlfriend (who is actually quite nice, I have to admit), and *then* he lets his girlfriend's *dog* come over and spend the evening with us.'

And this was the man who was once famous for his hatred of all things four-legged and furry, and who had not spoken to anyone who was not to do with work, my school or my friends since, like, forever.

'Dog?' said Jaffa, shivering slightly. 'Jaffsie not sure she like a big woofy doggy to come here.'

I smiled and hugged her. 'Don't worry, you'll love Sparky. He's cute and he wouldn't hurt a fly.'

Best not to mention the fact that he likes chasing small furry animals, I thought.

'Mmm. Me is hoping Bertie is right about this,' Jaffa said in a small voice, fitting herself into my arms in a tight ball.

'The whole reason Sparky is coming is to protect you,' I tried to reassure her. 'Think of him as your own personal guard dog.'

Jaffa looked at me in horror. 'What does Bertie mean, "*guard* dog"?' she asked, stiff with fright.

'Hey, hey, what's the matter?' I cooed. 'I'm just trying to help, you know.'

'Bertie must not let no dog do no guarding of Jaffsie! Nobody nor nothing is allowed to see the . . . the . . . thing!' she stammered. 'Jaffsie be in big bad trouble!'

I lost my patience. 'Listen, Jaffa,' I said. 'I'm getting a bit fed up with this. What is this "thing" you're

going on about?' I waited for a response, but Jaffa had shrunk in on herself and was avoiding eye contact. I sighed loudly. 'So. You see? If you won't talk to me, you'll have to let me work this out my way. And I reckon Bex has come up with a brilliant plan actually. If Sparky sees anything, he can show it his teeth and bark at it loudly. Then it'll get a fright, won't it? And serve it right.'

I was getting so worked up thinking about this mystery creature getting its just deserts that I hadn't noticed the effect of my words on Jaffa. Her hackles had risen, her eyes were wider than I'd ever seen them and her back was arched. 'TEETH?' she hissed. 'Me is not having nobody else with big teeth comin' in my house!'

'Nobody else?' I said quickly. 'What do you mean, 'nobody *else*'?'

'I mean, not nobody,' said Jaffa stubbornly.

I shook my head in bewilderment. 'I really don't know what you're on about,' I persisted, forcing myself to sound firm, 'but I'm afraid you *are* going to have to put up with Sparky coming, because otherwise we're in danger of being separated, you and me – for good.'

'What?' Jaffsie cried, jabbing me painfully with her tiny claws.

'Yes,' I said. I pushed her off me and rubbed my arm. 'Dad has had enough. If you don't tell us what's going on, we're going to have to solve it our way, and if you don't let us do that, Dad wants you to leave.'

I was overdoing it, of course. Dad hadn't actually said that, and if he did, I would put up a massive fight – I'd never let him send Jaffa away. And I knew deep down that he was too much of a softie to do that anyway. But I had to shock Jaffsie somehow – get her to see how serious we were about catching the offender she was mysteriously protecting. I

couldn't have her hitching any more lifts to school as a rucksack-stowaway.

'Me can't leave! Me can't go outside!' she whined. 'Not now, not never! Me is not never going outside again in my whole life! There's nasties out there!'

Blimey, things were obviously worse than I'd realized. I held her up so I could get a good look at her, face to face.

'Listen, Jaffsie. I am not going to *let* Dad chuck you out, OK? But you have to see that life is pretty difficult at the moment. And until we find out what's going on, or at least frighten this other creature away, life is not going to get any better, is it? You do see that, don't you?' I pleaded.

Jaffa went completely limp in my hands and started slipping. I clung on. 'Oh no, you don't!' I cried, grappling with my slithery cat, who seemed to have transformed herself into a piece of silk. 'You are not going to go and hide until I have your word that you'll at least let Sparky have a go at this thing!' I insisted.

Jaffa stopped struggling and gave me a look of such misery that I felt as though I had turned into an ogre. 'All right,' she said in a low voice. 'But I is telling you, Bertie, no one is going to make that monster frighted. It is not going to be frighted of no one, not never. Not even that big-teethed doggy.'

10

Guard Dog

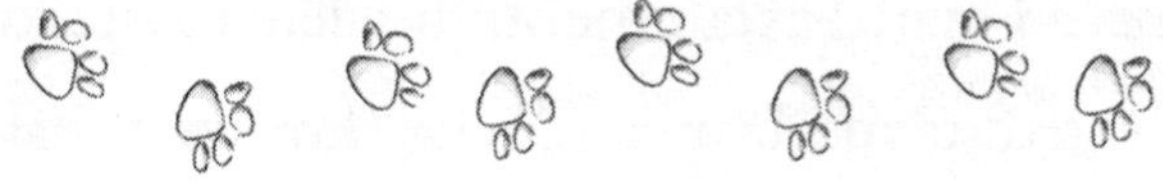

Friday took its time arriving. The rest of the week had dragged its feet like the slowest sloth in the jungle. I had tried to throw myself into other stuff, finding out about clubs and extra activities I could join in with to distract myself from thinking about the mystery beast. Not to mention to stop me being paranoid about Jazz and Fergus's new obsession with the Cool Gang, aka Kezia and Charlie. Whenever I spotted one of my friends in the crowded corridors I couldn't get near them; those two witches or one of their weird groupies were always in the way. And when I did get a moment with Jazz, all she could talk about was the auditions on Friday night.

'I've decided I'm going to design my own outfit this time!' she told me breathlessly. She was shiny-eyed with excitement. 'I need to stand out from the crowd. I mean, who knows what the competition will look like?'

I stopped listening to her after a while. I couldn't concentrate on what she was saying about how many hours she'd spent in her room practising new routines and downloading music. I was far too worried about my kitten. Jazz was on her own in this audition: I had my own agenda on Friday.

Bex came round at teatime with a very overexcited Sparky in tow. When I opened the door he was straining on the lead so hard that his thick orange collar was cutting into his fur and his tongue was lolling out of his mouth as he panted loudly. It seemed he had a desperate urge to get into the house as fast as possible.

'Sparky! Heel!' Bex said forcefully.

But Sparky had gone momentarily deaf.

'I'm sorry, Bertie,' she said, her face creased with concern. 'I think he can smell Jaffa, you see. He does get a bit worked up at new smells.'

I felt my face go tight with worry and Bex noticed. 'It's OK,' she said hurriedly. 'He wouldn't hurt—'

'A fly, I know,' I said, unconvinced. 'Come in,' I added, raising my voice above Sparky's rasping and panting.

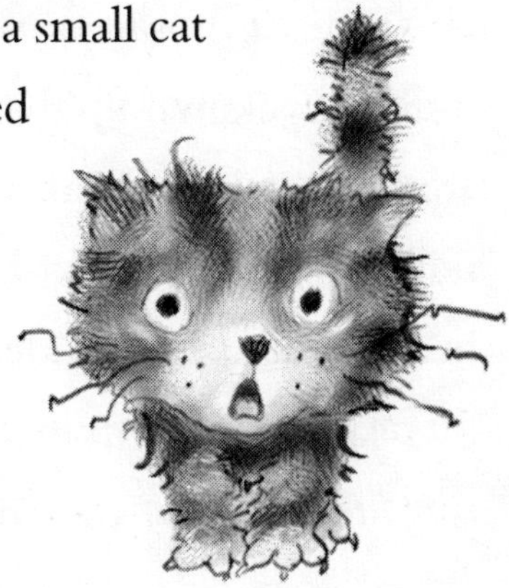

I turned to go into the house and caught a glimpse of Jaffa on the stairs. She looked about as horrified as it is possible for a small cat to look: her back was arched so high she was on tiptoes (or should that be tip-claws?) and her fur was sticking out all over the place as if someone had just rubbed her with a balloon and made her go all static. Her eyes were wide with terror and her mouth was pulled back to reveal her teeth as she hissed and spat for all she was worth.

'Nasty doggy!' she was shouting. 'Horrid, filthy beastie!'

'Jaffsie!' I reprimanded her.

'My word!' Bex exclaimed. 'I'd say someone's a bit put out!'

'Let's, er, go through, shall we?' I said, almost pushing Bex and Sparky down the hall to the kitchen. 'I'll settle Jaffa in my room and then we can set Sparky up with his bed and stuff. *Dad!*' I called.

Dad came out of the kitchen to welcome Bex while I rocketed up the stairs and cupped my hands around the bundle of spitting fury that was my kitten before she could take it into her tiny orange head to disappear under a wardrobe somewhere.

'Jaffsie is not likin' that nasty doggy!' she hissed.

'You've got to trust me on this,' I urged. 'I

won't let Sparky anywhere near you. You can stay in my room all night – I'll even bring you your tea. Meanwhile Sparky will guard the back door, and if anything even *tries* to get in, he will deal with it. By this time tomorrow, there will be no more nasty doggy, and, more importantly, no more nasty scary monster taking your food and making a mess, OK?'

At last Jaffa stopped hissing and put her claws away. I fetched a soft plumped-up cushion and put it in the middle of my bed and told her it was a special cushion just for her. Then I promised I'd be up a little later to check on her. I think she must have worn herself out, because as soon as she'd got herself comfy on the cushion she curled up in a ball, tucking her head under her tail, and fell asleep.

I had a sudden unwelcome thought as I was going down the stairs: what if Dad and Bex were having a cuddle? It would be excruciatingly embarrassing if I walked in on them. I supposed they did kiss and cuddle – that was what boyfriends and girlfriends did, wasn't it? Even if they were old? It made me shudder. I mean, I wanted Dad to be happy and everything, but I couldn't help feeling it would all be a lot easier if Bex was just a good friend.

I decided that the only thing to do was to give them fair warning that I was coming, so that if they *were* having a cuddle they would have time to stop before I entered the room. So I started coughing really loudly and singing the first song which came into my head, which unfortunately was, 'Who let the dogs out? Woof! Woof! Woof-woof!' How totally weird can you get?

I needn't have worried. Bex and Dad were sitting at the table, drinking coffee and chatting quietly, and Sparky was curled up at their feet. Until he heard me, that is. He leaped up as I entered the kitchen and banged his head on the table and then started barking and slobbering all over again.

'Are you all right?' Dad asked, over the racket Sparky was creating. He peered at me curiously. 'You weren't coughing like that earlier. I hope you're not getting a cold so early on in the term.'

'Not a great choice of song either!' Bex said wearily. 'Down, Sparky!' she commanded, shooting her dog a scarily withering look, which silenced him immediately. He put his tail between his legs, lowered his head in an impressively shameful expression, and crawled back to his place under the table, whimpering quietly.

'Wow,' said Dad in mock admiration. 'I wouldn't want to get on the wrong side of you.'

'No chance of that. Tee-hee!' said Bex, batting her eyelashes at him.

Get me a bucket, I thought. But I just coughed again and said, 'Ahem! Shall we move Sparky into the utility room now?'

Bex managed to drag her eyes away from Dad for a millisecond and said, 'Yeah, sure. We'll sort out your intruder problem once and for all, won't we, Sparky-boy?'

Sparky did not take kindly to being shut in the utility room, especially when he smelt the delicious creamy chicken curry Bex was cooking for tea, and he whined when we shut the door on him. But he soon quietened down and we heard him snuffling around the room for the treats Bex had hidden for him.

We took our plates into the sitting room and got comfy on the sofa, all three of us in a row. Bex had brought round a DVD about a couple who got a dog who was really badly behaved, but who they loved to bits. It was hilarious the kinds of things the dog got up to – like diving out of the car window while the couple were driving along, chasing a cat over all the fences in the neighbourhood, and crashing into everyone's parties and barbecues and even into someone's swimming pool. I was really

enjoying it and it certainly took my mind off Jaffa.

Then out of the blue, the film turned into a romantic comedy! There was this toe-curlingly awful bit where the couple actually started *kissing*. URGH and double-URGH! I could almost *feel* Dad and Bex thinking lovey-dovey thoughts towards each other. I closed my eyes, scrunched my toes up inside my slippers and sat on my hands, tensing my arm away from Dad and wishing the sofa would swallow me up.

CRASH!

SQUEAL!

HOOOOOOWWWL!

What a racket . . . I opened one eye to see what was going on. But it wasn't the dog in the film who was making the noise.

HOOOOOWWWWL!

'Sparky?' Bex had leaped from the sofa and was dashing towards the kitchen, where it sounded like a herd of elephants had crashed into the house, knocking a few doors down and a few bits of furniture besides.

'What the . . . ?' Dad jumped up as well, knocking over his empty plate and sending his drink flying.

I followed as Bex shouted, 'Sparky! Sparky? Are you all right, boy? It's OK, Mummy's coming!'

By the time I got to the utility room, Bex was sitting on the floor, cradling the poor pooch in her arms, her cheeks wet with tears. The room was a total bomb site. Even the events of the past few days hadn't prepared me for this level of devastation. The ceiling light was swinging to and fro as if something had been hanging from it, cupboard doors were teetering on their hinges, and every available surface was covered in cleaning products, cat food, washing powder and damp laundry.

But none of this was as bad as what had happened to poor old Sparky. He had blood trickling from a gash on his face and he was whimpering in

fright, cowering in Bex's arms as though he'd just seen a ghost. Or a monster.

'This is worse than we thought,' Dad said grimly. 'I've a good mind to call the police.'

Bex shook her head, and said through her tears, 'No point. It must be a wild animal. A fox or something.'

'Oh, Sparky,' I said sorrowfully. 'I'm so sorry, boy.'

'At least we know it's not Jaffa,' said Bex, putting on a brave smile.

'That's true,' said Dad. 'From the looks of poor Sparky here I have to say she's had a narrow escape so far. We're going to have to block up the cat flap to keep Jaffa safe.'

Too right, I thought. And she's going to have to talk to me now, surely. If the intruder was vicious enough to upset Sparky this much, we had to find out who or what it was.

11

A Walk in the Park

The next morning I had a lie-in, relieved it was Saturday at last. When I woke up it took a minute for me to recall what had happened the night before. I lifted my head and was comforted to see Jaffa sleeping soundly, curled into a neat comma at the foot of my bed. I lay back, replaying in my mind the noises Sparky had made, and shuddering at the memory. I knew Dad was probably right about keeping the cat flap locked. But the longer I lay there, staring at the ceiling, the more I felt myself needing to know who or what this intruder was, rather than simply shutting it out. I owed it to my little kitten to get rid of this monster once and

for all, if only to make it up to her for not believing her in the first place, when she had insisted she was not to blame.

I got up and took a shower, the water as hot as I could stand it, the roar of it filling my ears. I fumbled with the slippery shampoo bottle and washed my hair vigorously. So how was I going to catch the culprit and teach it a lesson? The only way I could think of solving this was to stay up all night, camped out in the kitchen.

Yeah, like Dad was going to let me do that, I thought, wincing as shampoo trickled into my eyes. Come to think of it, I wasn't sure I wanted to anyway. If Sparky had been scared out of his wits, what's to say I wouldn't be too? I pictured the nasty scratch he had received and winced again.

I towelled my hair dry and pulled on some jeans and a T-shirt – ah, the bliss of not having to wear that uniform! My mobile was flashing; I assumed Jazz had sent me a text telling me how the auditions had gone. But it was Fergus.

Hey! Missed you yesterday. Wanna come round?

My heart did a funny fluttery skip-and-a-hop into my throat. It would be good to have a chance to spend time with Fergus without Kezia around.

'Da-ad!' I yelled as I hurtled downstairs.

Silence.

He wouldn't have left the house without waking me, would he? I called again as I made my way down the hall.

He hadn't gone out. He was standing in the middle of the kitchen, a mop in one hand, a bucket in the other. He looked at me grimly.

'Oh no . . .' I whispered, shaking my head.

'Oh yes, I'm afraid so,' Dad said.

'But you locked the cat flap, I saw you,' I protested.

'Unfortunately it seems our intruder is not put off by the simple addition of a lock,' he said. He

gestured with his head towards the utility room. 'Take a look.'

'Oh . . . !' My skin prickled horribly as I stared at what had once been a fully functioning cat flap. The plastic door was hanging loosely by a thread, and the red lock had popped off and was lying pathetically on the floor.

Dad had followed me in. 'Thank goodness Jaffa was sleeping on your bed last night,' he said. 'I dread to think what the . . . whatever-it-is would have done if it had got hold of her after bashing its way in here. All I can say is, it must be really desperate, because there's blood on the flap, look!'

I took a step nearer and saw that Dad was right: red streaks stained the edge of the plastic door. The creature had hurt itself, and I'm ashamed to say that I was almost pleased. Served it right if it was going to come crashing into our home, terrorizing my kitten, stealing her food and even attacking poor Sparky.

'What are we going to do, Bertie?' he asked, running his hand through his already ruffled hair. 'At least the whatever-it-is hasn't been able to get upstairs. I don't much fancy our chances against it either!'

I shuddered. 'We need help, that's for sure,' I said. 'I was just going to go over to Fergus's after breakfast. I'll ask him if he's got any ideas. Remember they used to have a cat, so maybe they've gone through this kind of thing too.'

'Hmm,' said Dad doubtfully. 'Worth a try, I suppose. Where's Jaffa now, by the way?'

'Still shut in my room.'

'Best place for her for now,' Dad said. 'Right, well, I'd better get on. I'm taking Bex out shopping,' he said, suddenly looking sheepish. 'You don't mind, do you?'

I grinned. 'No, Dad. I don't mind.' I gave him a hug. 'I like Bex, you know that. She's nice. And she's been brilliant with Jaffsie.' I guiltily recalled

her mercy dash to school earlier in the week – for my benefit she had even kept that from Dad. 'I'll either be at Fergus's or round at Jazz's place. See you later.'

After munching my way through a piece of toast, I quickly texted Fergus to say I was on my way. Then I hunted out a pair of trainers and pulled them on.

Another good thing about Dad spending time with Bex, I thought as I crossed the road to number 15, was that he was too wrapped up in his own life to tease me about Fergus any more. When I first met Fergus, Dad was always flashing me a cheeky grin and raising his eyebrows knowingly whenever I mentioned his name. I had worked out quite a while ago that the best way of dealing with this kind of behaviour was to shoot Dad a particularly withering look and then turn my back on him, but now I didn't even need to bother.

I rang the doorbell, quickly running my hands

through my hair, squaring my shoulders and holding my head high. Not for Fergus's benefit, by the way. It was Fiona, his mum, who made me feel like a total scruff-bag. She and I got on well enough these days, but she had this way of sizing me up, looking me up and down with a slightly sniffy air to check out what I was wearing. This irritated me as well as making me feel uncomfortable, as until I'd met her I'd never been bothered about being scruffy: it was just the way I was. But she was always so immaculate. I was convinced she looked perfect even when she woke up first thing in the morning. Maybe she slept on her back with her hands by her sides, like Sleeping Beauty, and didn't move a muscle all night . . .

I was biting back a smirk at this image when the door opened. It was Fergus's dad.

'Oh, hi!' I said, knocked off balance. I hadn't expected Gavin to be at home. He was away so much with his work that I hadn't seen him for ages.

He was in the music business, a fact Jazz had been ultra-speedy in wheedling out of Fergus when they had first met. He had always seemed lovely – friendly and cheery, and quiet too. (Not much like his wife!) I had long ago decided that Fergus might *look* a lot like Fiona, but he had definitely got his personality from his dad.

'Hello, Bertie,' he said, his face lighting up with a warm smile. 'Lovely to see you! I'll call Fergus. He's listening to music in his room – probably got his headphones on with the volume turned up so loud he won't have heard the door!'

At that moment, Fiona came clip-clopping down the hall on her dainty heels, saying, 'What is it, Gavin darling? I've got to shoot out in a sec to see that— oh, it's you, Bertie darling,' she said, catching sight of me just in time to plaster on one of her children's-TV-presenter smiles. 'Come in, come in.' She stiffly held out one arm in as welcoming a gesture as I was ever likely to get from her and looked pointedly at my trainers. I took them off and left them neatly by the mat, as was expected of anyone who entered the hallowed shrine of Mrs Fiona Neat-as-a Pin Meerley.

Gavin rolled his eyes at me from behind his wife's back and then winked.

Fiona showed me into her pristine monochrome sitting room. Not for the first time this habit of hers struck me as rather formal – at my house everyone automatically headed for the kitchen. I sat down nervously on the edge of one of the white armchairs, anxious as always to avoid leaving any mark. As I fiddled with the hem of my T-shirt, Fiona arranged herself neatly on a white sofa opposite me, patting the seat next to her for me to come and join her. She was rather like a cat herself, I thought, as I watched her smooth her already perfectly coiffed hair and arrange her skirt. I shyly moved to sit beside her.

'So,' she said crisply, 'how would you say

Fergie is getting on at school?'

What? Wow, how to make a girl feel uncomfortable in one quick and easy step . . .

'Erm, OK . . . I guess,' I mumbled, staring at my knees. 'I haven't really seen that much of him, what with us being in different years.'

'Well, I hope he's actually going to do some work this term,' she said sharply. 'He seems to be spending all his time playing with this band. Ah, there you are, darling!' she said, turning to the door.

Saved! I thought, the panic that had been rising in me easing at the sight of Fergus scuffing his socked feet against the carpet.

'Hey,' said Fergus quietly.

'Hey,' I said, willing his mum to go.

'Right.' Fiona stood up briskly as if reading my thoughts, and brushed down her skirt. 'I'll have to leave you two to it; I'm already late.' She glanced at her watch and bustled out of the room.

Fergus raised his eyebrows and waited until his mum was out of earshot. 'Sorry about that,' he said. 'Hope she wasn't hassling you.'

'No – checking up on you, actually!'

'Oh?' said Fergus, frowning slightly.

'No, really – I'm just joking,' I said quickly. Doh! What had I said that for?

'OK, so . . . do you want to go out?' he said.

We decided to head to the park, and on the way Fergus told me about the band and how he was really chuffed Kezia had told him about it. 'Not sure what I think of her though,' he added awkwardly. 'She's a bit . . . bossy!'

A warm sensation spread in my chest. 'Yeah?' I said. I was careful to keep my voice as uninterested as possible.

'Mmm – kind of like Jazz on a *really* hyper day!' he said, glancing across at me and grinning.

'That reminds me,' I said. 'Did you go to those auditions yesterday for the show?'

Fergus looked at me blankly. 'What show?'

'You know – the one Kezia and Charlie are organizing for the end of term. They roped Jazz in – not that they had to try very hard, as you can imagine! She was well up for it. She hasn't stopped going on about it – don't tell me you hadn't noticed?'

Fergus was pulling a face and shaking his head. 'Don't know what you're talking about,' he said. 'There weren't any auditions. Anyway, I can't see Kez organizing a show. Rashid reckons she's got as much musical talent as a cat playing the violin!'

His mention of the word cat reminded me why I'd been so keen to talk to him.

'Talking of cats . . .' I began.

'Oh yeah! How's Jaffsie? Man, I should've come round to yours this morning instead of dragging you over to ours to be interrogated by Mum. It's ages since I've seen that crazy little scruff-ball.'

'Hey! Who are you calling a scruff-ball?' I said in mock indignation.

We had arrived at the park. 'Put it this way – she's a lot like her owner,' said Fergus. Then, flashing me an evil grin, he shouted, 'Race you to the swings!' and charged off, his long legs giving him an unfair advantage. I chased after him, giggling and shouting at him to stop.

I skidded to a halt as Fergus plonked himself down on one of the swings and kicked himself off the ground. I dodged his legs and grabbed the swing next to him. Soon we were arcing through the air in tandem and shouting a conversation across to each other. Fergus howled with laughter when I told him that Jaffa had managed to hitch a ride to school with me – 'So that's why you were acting so weird!' – and then looked grim as I gave him all the details about Sparky, finishing with the monster-through-the-cat-flap episode. He had stopped kicking and leaning back by this point and

was letting the swing slowly come to a standstill.

When I'd finished he let out a long, low whistle and said, 'Why didn't you tell me all this before? You know I would've been, like, happy to help.'

I shrugged, feeling my face grow hot. 'You've been kind of busy.'

Fergus looked ashamed. 'I'm sorry,' he said softly. 'I . . . I didn't even think you'd want to hang out with me that much at school, to be honest. I thought you'd have tons of friends in your own year from your last school. And, well, I guess I've been trying to make friends in my own year too. And then there's the band—'

'It's OK!' I said. 'I don't expect you to look after me.'

Fergus looked stung. 'Right.'

I immediately felt bad and started babbling. 'So, any ideas how to get rid of the mystery marauder? Dad's freaking out and threatening to keep Jaffa under permanent house arrest. Either that, or I reckon he might even make me get rid of her.'

My voice caught in my throat as I said those last words.

Fergus at once reached out and laid a hand on my arm. 'No! He won't do that. I won't let him!' he said rashly. He was silent for a moment. Then his expression began subtly to change from ultra-anxious via thoughtful through to I've-just-had-a-brainwave. His dark blue eyes flashed excitedly and he gasped.

'You know what?' he said. 'I think I've just come up with the perfect solution.'

'Yes?' I asked. I felt a surge of hope wash over my gloomy thoughts.

'Cameras!' he said.

'What?'

'Cameras!' he repeated. He leaped off the swing, sending it rattling chaotically to and fro, and stood in front of me, waving his hands about like a loon. 'The way to catch the monster is to rig up a

camera in your utility room! Mum works in telly, right? So she's got access to some pretty funky technology. Leave it with me. I'm sure she'll want to help. You know how much she loves Jaffa,' he said mischievously.

I rolled my eyes, but I was grinning my head off. I had to admit, it was a pretty cool plan. I just hoped Fergus was right about his mum wanting to help.

12

Something's Up

Once we'd said our goodbyes, I thought about calling in on Jazz to tell her about Fergus's genius idea. Even though Jazz had never cared that much about my pet, or anyone else's for that matter (and that included her little brother's guinea pig, Huckleberry), I knew that she would prick up her ears at the mention of the words 'filming' and 'camera'.

As I rang the bell, I realized Jazz hadn't replied to any of my texts. I'd texted her a few times since Friday . . . Weird, I thought. She couldn't have lost her phone *again*, surely? Still, phone or no phone, she had been so hyper about the auditions

it wouldn't be altogether surprising if she had forgotten I existed. Then I remembered what Fergus had said about there not *being* any auditions. There was an uneasy niggling sensation at the back of my mind, as though a voice was trying to warn me about something.

I heard footsteps pattering down the hall. It was Jazz's little brother, Tyson, who had come to greet me. As soon as he flung the door open with his characteristic energy I was hit by a wall of sound. The usual Brown Family Rumpus was going on inside: Jazz's mum was yelling at someone, someone was yelling back, horrendous music was thumping through the ceiling and a strange smell accompanied by rather a lot of smoke was coming out of the kitchen.

'Hi,' said Tyson calmly.

'Like the T-shirt,' I said, raising an eyebrow at his orange and green top; it had the words 'Weapon of Mass Destruction' written across the front.

'Cool, innit?' Ty squeaked, jumping up and down suddenly for no apparent reason. 'Sam sent it from New York.'

Sam was the oldest Brown child – though he wasn't a child any more. He had just left uni and was spending a year in the States doing something 'totally boring' according to Jazz. Jazz had an older sister too – Aleisha. She still lived at home, but wasn't around much.

'So,' I said, 'any chance I could come in?'

'Oh. Yeah,' said Ty, still bouncing. He moved to one side and, filling his lungs, he yelled, 'JA-A-A-A-ZZ! BERTIE'S HERE!'

The shrieking at the other end of the house stopped abruptly and Mrs Brown came out of the kitchen, looking very unlike her normal unflustered self. Her face had smudges on it, her forehead was creased into a frown and her hair was rather ruffled.

She tried to smile. 'Hello, Bertie. Perhaps you

can talk some sanity into my daughter. Even her father and Aleisha don't seem to be getting through to her.'

Jazz was flailing down the hall behind her mum, shouting, 'It's just not fair! You don't understand me! I HATE you!'

Even for Jazz, this was pretty strong stuff.

Mrs Brown whirled round on the spot and sucked her teeth harshly. She stood her ground in front of Jazz, towering over her and staring her down. Jazz immediately shrank about ten centimetres.

'I think,' her mother said in a dangerously cold voice, 'you had better apologize, young lady.'

'Sorr-*eee*.'

'Fine. Now go up to your room and turn that appalling racket off. Bertie can go with you. You and I will talk later.'

Jazz made a point of staring at a mark on the wall to the left of her mum and tried to keep her face set in a defiant expression, but it was clear that she had already lost this particular battle.

'Whatever,' she said. But very quietly.

The last thing I wanted was to stay in their house while the atmosphere had the flavour of a war zone about it, but I had gone and got myself invited in now. So there was no getting out of it. In any case, part of me was a bit curious as to what the row had been about.

'What's going on?' I said as I followed Jazz into her room.

Jazz turned and scowled at me. 'Like *you* care,' she said.

'Er, like, yes, I so *do*,' I said, mimicking her sarcastic tone.

Jazz pushed open her door and went over to where her iPod was fixed on a massive docking station – a recent present from Sam which Mrs Brown had not been overly pleased about due to the size of the speakers. She whacked the volume

up a couple of notches, but swiftly flicked it back down when her mum started yelling again from the hall.

Jazz flumped on to her beanbag and folded her arms tightly, sticking out her bottom lip in a furious pout.

'So,' I said, sitting down on the floor opposite her and crossing my legs, 'you OK? Only, it seems, as you would say, a tad *stressy* round here today. And what's with you ignoring my texts?'

'Like I said, do you really care? Seems to me like you and Fergus are so *loved-up* these days you couldn't give a stuff about anyone else,' she snarled.

'Whoa!' I cried, throwing up my hands in front of my face. Her tone was laced with so much acid, I felt physically stung. 'For your information, Fergus and I are not "loved-up", and as for me giving a stuff about anyone else, I could say the same to you!'

Jazz's face immediately crumpled and she buried it in her hands. I noted with alarm that her shoulders were shaking.

'Jazz?' I said sharply, shuffling over to squeeze next to her. I put a tentative arm around her.

She shrugged me off and shifted slightly away.

'Jazz! I'm sorry I shouted at you, OK? You're obviously upset. Tell me what's going on, please?' I felt panic rising up in me. My best friend never cried.

She peered through her braided hair, mascara-tears streaking her cheeks. 'You'll only say, "I told you so."'

I narrowed my eyes and shook my head. 'Why would I do that?' Then I stopped short. 'Oh, Jazz – it's not the auditions, is it?'

Jazz hesitated for a split second and then said sullenly, 'No.'

I bit my lip. 'Are you sure? Fergus reckoned . . .' I stopped myself. Not a good idea to mention

Fergus after what she'd just said about us. 'Well, it must be something pretty important,' I persisted. 'You don't usually shout at your mum quite like that, and I've never seen you in such a state.'

Jazz wiped her eyes and nose on the sleeve of her purple and silver T-shirt and snapped, 'I'm just not having a ball at the moment, OK? And I don't really want to talk about it. So can we change the subject?'

I breathed deeply, forcing myself to think of something that might lighten the mood. Then I remembered Fergus's plan and I said, 'Hey! How do you fancy getting involved in some undercover work?'

'Eh?'

'A covert operation to catch a mystery intruder,' I said, laying on the suspense. I wiggled my eyebrows and twirled a fake moustache as if I were a mad detective.

Jazz sniggered in spite of herself. 'You are a

nuthead,' she said. 'What are you on about?'

'First of all, I have to tell you what's been going on round at my place . . .' I told Jazz the whole story, just as I had earlier to Fergus. I finished by saying, 'So you see, that's why I've been pretty distracted. Not because I'm "loved-up". And in any case, Fergus has been busy too.' I risked saying his name again, cautiously watching out for any sign of Jazz launching into another tirade. She didn't react, so I went on, 'He's either hanging out with Rashid and the guys in the band, or he's surrounded by Kezia and her too-cool-for-school mates.'

Jazz gave a little shiver. That was the worst bit about crying, I thought. Once you'd stopped sobbing you had to go through that cold, shuddery stage when your eyes felt raw and your nose dripped with snot.

I got up to fetch her a tissue from a box on her desk.

'So what's this got to do with a "covert thing-

ummy"?' Jazz asked, taking the tissue and blowing her nose.

'Oh, sorry! Yeah, erm, well, Fergus came up with this idea to catch Jaffa's torturer on camera,' I said.

Jazz's eyes regained some of their usual sparkle as I filled her in. 'That sounds cool!' she said, a smile playing around the corners of her mouth. 'D'you reckon Fiona will go for it?'

'Let's hope so,' I said. 'Then you can come over and watch the action!'

Jazz beamed, her sore eyes crinkling at the edges. 'Fab!'

'In the meantime – fancy cracking on with some of that horrendous homework? It's got to be better doing it together,' I said.

Jazz groaned. 'If we have to,' she said, rolling her eyes.

I smiled, glad to see my friend behaving a bit more like normal.

'Mates?' I said.

'Mates,' she agreed, giving me a hug.

But somehow I was still feeling uneasy. Jazz was definitely not herself.

13

Plan Number Two

Jazz asked her mum if she could do her homework at my place; unsurprisingly Mrs Brown seemed only too glad to see the back of her stroppy daughter for a couple of hours. While Jazz gathered up her books, I asked her mum if it would be all right for Jazz to stay for a sleepover too.

'Thanks, Bertie,' she said. 'That would be great. Anything to put a smile on that girl's face,' she added. 'She's been nothing but hard work ever since starting the new school. You don't know if anything's happened, do you?'

What was this? First it was Fiona, checking up on Fergus, and now Jazz's mum was quizzing

me about *her* daughter! Was I the neighbourhood agony aunt or something?

Taking a deep breath, I explained that I hadn't seen much of Jazz. 'We don't have all our classes together, and the days are so manic,' I said. 'And she's pretty busy with street dance and stuff,' I pointed out.

'Hmm,' said Mrs Brown thoughtfully. 'Well, I just hope you girls don't drift apart. You've been friends for too long,' she said sadly.

I smiled reassuringly. 'We'll always be friends, me and Jazz, don't you worry.'

We had a laugh that afternoon. We holed up in my room with our homework scattered all over the floor, put some music on low (to help us concentrate, you understand) and brought a pile of snacks from the kitchen to sustain us. Jaffa was still shut in my room, to be on the safe side, and she padded to and fro the whole time, chattering away to me and distracting me by walking up and down my back,

kneading me through the fabric of my T-shirt with her tiny paws. We waded through the science, maths and geography we'd been given, breaking off every so often to gossip about the people in our classes and about how sad most of the teachers were. It almost felt as though life had got back to normal.

'That Mr Lloyd!' Jazz shrieked, flapping her hands and jumping up and down in hysterics. 'He dresses like my *grandad*! No, he dresses like my *grandad's* grandad!'

'Oh boy! And that Miss Stoodge,' I joined in. 'What a witch!'

We had given up on the last bit of work and were rolling around on the floor, tickling Jaffa and singing along to the music we had cranked up on my ancient CD player, when Dad knocked on my door. 'I can see you two girls are working hard!' he teased. 'Just thought I'd let you know I'm back. No activity downstairs while I was away?' he asked.

'No,' I said. 'Oh, but Dad – Fergus thinks he

might have come up with a way of catching the culprit!' I cried.

Dad tried to look doubtful by crossing his arms. 'So he reckons he can succeed where others have failed, does he?' he said dramatically. He was smiling though. 'I have to say it would be nice to have a quiet evening with no mention of intruders for once. Bex is coming round later with some food – do you want to stay and eat with us, Jazz?' he added. 'We haven't seen much of you lately.'

Jazz nodded enthusiastically. 'Yes, please!'

'Can Fergus come round too?' I asked. I put on a pleading expression, wringing my hands, making myself look as desperate as possible. 'I really want you to hear his plan –'

Before Dad could answer, there was a ring at the front door. 'I'll get that,' said Dad. Then he fixed me with a mock-stern stare and pointed his finger, saying, 'And just so we're clear, I have not said yes to anything yet, Bertie Fletcher!'

I shrugged and tried to look as if butter wouldn't melt in my mouth as he turned to go back downstairs.

Jazz and I sped out on to the landing and peered over the banisters to see who it was.

'Nigel!' Fiona's crystal-clear voice carried up the stairs.

'Ah, hello, Fiona,' said Dad. 'And Fergus too! What a surprise,' he said with an edge of sarcasm, casting his eyes in my direction. 'Come in, come in.'

'It the prawn-lady!' Jaffa mewed excitedly. 'Me want to say hello!' I scooped her up into my arms and Jazz and I rattled down to the hall.

Wonders will never cease, as Dad says on the rare occasions that I tidy my room without being asked. But in this case the wonders were in the region of the unbelievably miraculous: Fiona Meerley, the woman whom only months earlier I had been ready to write off as my own worst enemy, had not only agreed to Fergus's idea, but had also pulled out all the stops and arranged to get the equipment we needed for that very night!

'You know how much I *adore* the little pusskins,' she cooed. 'I'd do anything to stop her being bullied in this beastly way.' She bent down to stroke my kitten's soft orangey fur while making the sort of kissy-wissy sounds that frankly turned my stomach.

Fergus, Jazz and I exchanged smirks while Jaffa lapped up the attention, purring noisily. She closed her eyes in a satisfied expression that made it look as if she was smiling. 'Me *is* pretty adorable,' she admitted.

'So, about this plan of yours. Run me through the details?' Dad said as he poured coffee into mugs

and went to the fridge for milk.

Fiona cleared her throat and said, 'A covert surveillance operation.'

'Sorry?' Dad turned to face her, the milk carton in one hand, his face creased in puzzlement.

'It's like in those films—' Fergus began, but Fiona interrupted him.

'Surveillance,' she repeated. 'Mark my words, we will catch this intruder red-handed – or should I say red-pawed! Ha!' She let out a short sharp bark of a laugh. It was the first time I had ever heard her laugh, or make an attempt at humour, for that matter. As laughs go, it was pretty scary.

Fergus grimaced.

Dad gave a nervous snigger. 'The thing is, Fiona, the whatever-it-is comes when no one else is around, so surely if we piled into the utility room waiting for it, it would know we were there and stay away.'

'Aaah, that's where a bit of creative thinking

comes in, Nigel,' Fiona said in crisp and efficient tones. 'Thanks to my job, I have considerable experience in catching people unawares – on camera.' She paused for effect, leaning back against the kitchen worktop and cradling her steaming mug of coffee.

'Oh. My. Goodness!' squealed Jazz. 'You really are going to bring, like, a *totally live camera crew* into this house?'

Fiona arched one eyebrow. 'Not an entire crew, Jasmeena, no,' she said condescendingly. 'It would be a little . . . cramped. One man should do the job.'

'Wow,' said Dad doubtfully. 'So you can rig up something to record any activity in the utility room and—'

'—catch the culprit on film. Absolutely. Then we'll know exactly what we are dealing with and we'll be able to go from there,' Fiona finished.

Typical Fiona, I thought, stealing the limelight. This had been Fergus's idea, but she was doing all

the talking. I stole a glance at him, but he simply shrugged. Fiona did have a way of getting things to turn out just the way she wanted, I supposed, and if it meant we could put an end to Jaffa being bullied, then I was prepared to let her get away with it.

'I've already taken the liberty of checking I can get everything we need from work,' Fiona was saying. 'We have night-vision cameras, microphones, you name it. And I can get one of the technicians to come and set it up. I'm on extremely good terms with a chap who works on the *Naturewatch* series – they're always doing this kind of thing when they want to film animals in their natural habitat without disturbing them.'

Jazz started bouncing up and down on the spot, looking a whole lot like her younger brother, I thought. 'A telly guy! Here!' she kept saying, clapping her hands.

'Genius,' said Dad. He seemed at a loss for words.

Fiona nodded curtly. 'That's what I thought,' she said. 'So we'll come round in an hour. Nev said he should be free by then. It just so happens he was already filming in the area.'

'Nev? In an hour?' Dad repeated, looking pretty shell-shocked. He blinked and took his glasses off to clean them on the edge of his shirt. Then, finding his voice again, he mumbled, 'Er, I'm not sure we can do this tonight actually, Fiona. You see, my f-friend is coming round and—'

'Nonsense,' said Fiona, waving a dismissive hand.

Dad blew his cheeks out and shrugged, a look of complete surrender on his face.

'Fine,' he said eventually. 'Whatever. See you in an hour. With Nev,' he added. Then he looked at me as if to say, 'What on earth am I letting myself in for?'

14

Lights, Camera, Action!

Fiona and Fergus returned as promised an hour later. Bex had arrived by then as well, and was engaged in a heated debate with Jazz over the takeaway she had brought with her. (According to Jazz, takeaway is not takeaway unless you get to go to the place yourself, see the menu with your own eyes and choose it in person. She was not impressed that Bex had made the selection without consulting her.)

I couldn't help smiling to myself as Bex tried in vain to explain that she hadn't known Jazz was eating with us. I knew Jazz was being rude, but there was something reassuring about seeing my friend being her usual confident self.

'You so cannot have a curry without poppadoms!' Jazz said, her face contorted in outrage.

'OK, so next time I'll get poppadoms,' said Bex wearily.

'And you've not got that *rank* naan bread with raisins in? Urgh!' Jazz went on.

I left them battling it out and went to open the door. Fergus and Fiona were in the middle of an animated conversation with a man dressed in baggy combat trousers and an outsized brown jumper with frayed sleeves and holes in the elbows.

'Hi,' I said shyly.

Fiona looked up. 'Ah, Bertie. This is Nev Greenshield. From the *Naturewatch* team.'

'Hi,' said Nev. He was so tall I was worried I might get a stiff neck from looking up at him. He was really skinny too: all arms and legs like a daddy-long-legs. Maybe he wore such baggy clothes to hide how thin he was. He smiled warmly. I was

going to like Nev, I decided. He seemed like a real gentle giant.

'Come in,' I said, stepping aside. 'I'll get Dad.'

Nev had to stoop to avoid banging his head on the door frame. Fiona followed him and I stood there, waiting.

Fiona looked puzzled. 'You can shut the door now, Bertie. It's just us.'

'Oh, I, er . . . I thought you might want to bring all the equipment in,' I said, glancing out to see if they'd left any bags on the path.

Nev held up a black bag a bit like a bulky laptop case. 'All in here,' he said.

Jazz had joined us, still muttering about Bex having 'no idea' how to order a takeaway. She took one look at Nev and his little black bag and said, 'Is that it?'

I had to admit, it didn't look very impressive.

Fiona let out a tinkling laugh. 'Don't look so disappointed, dear. Nev knows what he's doing, I can assure you.'

Jazz curled her lip in disgust. 'Sure,' she said, hands on hips.

Fergus rolled his eyes. 'Jazz, she's right. Nev *does* know what he's doing.'

'This is all I normally use in the field,' Nev explained, thankfully unfazed by Jazz. 'I'll unpack and talk you through it, shall I?'

Dad finally emerged. 'Ah! You must be Nev – pleasure to meet you. I'm Nigel.' He beamed and held out his hand. Nev took it and pumped it up and down energetically. 'Come through into the kitchen. We're just sorting out some supper. There's plenty for everyone.'

We followed Dad into the kitchen, where Bex was laying out foil dishes of steaming food. She looked rather alarmed at the number of people who were crowding into the room, but did a quick headcount and went to get plates. Fergus and I busied ourselves sorting out drinks while Jazz pestered

Nev with questions about life as a cameraman. Fiona finished off most of Nev's sentences for him. Poor guy, I thought, looking over at him. Working with Fiona must be even worse than working with that bonkers bird-watching guy on the telly, the one with the beard as big as a golden eagle's nest and the temper like a wasps' nest.

Dad stepped in and offered some food round, prising Jazz away from Nev.

'I'll have something in a minute if that's OK,' Nev said. 'Let's get the gear sorted first.'

I was quite happy to leave the mayhem in the kitchen and go with Nev into the utility room.

'That's the cat flap – what's left of it!' I showed him the plastic door hanging limply from its frame.

'OK,' said Nev, checking out the room. 'I reckon if I fix the camera to the top of that cupboard and angle it at the cat flap . . .' He started fiddling around, moving things out of the way, stepping back to look through the lens, making adjustments, pressing buttons, and so on.

'Are you all right in here for a bit?' I asked. Nev nodded, not looking up from his gadgets.

I went to my room to find my kitten. I needed to tell her what was going on.

'Jaffsie!'

I scanned the room.

'Jaffa? Where are you?' Oh no, she hadn't gone and done one of her famous escapology routines, had she?

But then I heard a squeaking noise from across the landing. I tracked it down to Dad's study.

'Jaffa?'

My cheeky little cat was curled up on Dad's desk on top of a pile of papers: a cute, furry paper-weight.

'What are you doing in here?' I admonished. 'I shut you into my room to keep you safe.'

'Borin' in Bertie's room all the time!' she

mewed pitifully. 'Bertie's door was open a teeny-tiny bit, so me did get one little paw in the gap, and me did puuuush and puuuush and use all of me's strength and muscles and me did get out,' she explained proudly.

I sighed and shook my head.

She gave an exaggerated yawn in response, showing every one of her brilliant white teeth. Then she stretched back on to her hind legs, extending her front paws and flexing her little claws, rumpling a couple of the sheets of paper as she did so. As always, her gorgeousness made me tingle all over with love for her and I quickly pushed aside any feelings of irritation. I took a step towards her to pick her up for a snuggle, and she purred.

'Who is those noisy people downstairs? Me was havin' a lovely dream until they came,' she said, rubbing her head against my outstretched hand. 'Me was in a soft green place and there was mousies runnin' everywhere and me was chasin' them and bein' very brave.'

I giggled. 'You *are* very brave, little Jaffsie,' I crooned. 'But soon you won't have to be brave any more. Fergus and his mum are here with a nice man called Nev. He is setting up a camera so that when the big bad nasty thing comes back, we'll record it all and find out what it is.'

Jaffa stiffened. 'No!' she squeaked.

'What's the matter now?' I was really fed up. Here I was, doing everything I could think of to solve the problem of her being bullied, and not only was she being no help at all, she was positively trying to stop my plans.

'Me did tell you, me is not allowed for you to know who Big Bo— who the big baddie is,' she whined.

I had had enough of this. I set her down rather roughly on the desk and snapped, 'Well, you're just going to have to trust me on this.' Then I turned and walked out of the room, shutting the door

firmly behind me. She was not going to escape a second time.

Downstairs, Nev had finished setting up his equipment and he was tucking into some food while everyone else sat round the table, drinking coffee and chatting.

'Oh, there you are, love,' said Dad, smiling. 'Come and look at this.'

I grabbed some of the 'rank' naan bread (which I personally thought was lush) and followed Dad into the utility room. He beamed and pointed gleefully at a camera fixed to the top of the broom cupboard. 'Nifty, eh?' he said. 'And that's not the best bit,' he continued, taking me by the elbow and steering me back into the kitchen.

Nev was over by the kettle, looking at a lap-top.

'Check out what's onscreen,' said Dad, pointing at the computer.

I went over to Nev and saw that he was

looking at a picture of our utility room.

'Isn't that great?' Dad said. 'Our own home security system.'

Nev tapped a few keys and suddenly the image zoomed in on the cat flap. It was like watching something out of a spy movie, and I had to admit I was impressed.

'I'll go in there and you keep watching,' Dad said. He skipped out of the room like a small boy with a new toy, grinning excitedly.

I watched the screen and suddenly Dad appeared, waving and saying, 'Hello! Can you see me? Can you hear me?'

'I can hear you anyway, Dad. You're only next door,' I said scathingly.

But he was right, it was pretty cool. Then something occurred to me. 'What if the intruder is too fast for us to see what it is?' I asked Nev.

'No problem,' he said, tapping the keys again. The image of Dad slowed right down as though

he were walking on the moon. 'Slow-motion playback,' Nev said carelessly. 'It does it all, this little baby.'

If this lot didn't nail our mystery marauder, I thought, nothing would.

'You could also leave it something tempting to stop it in its tracks,' Nev suggested, with a twinkle in his eye. 'It's what I do when I want to lure badgers or foxes out of their holes so I can get a decent amount of footage,' he explained.

'Of course!' Dad said, snapping his fingers. 'Cat food – that's what the beast has been breaking in for all this time, isn't it?'

Nev shook his head. 'I was thinking of something totally irresistible, if you know what I mean.'

'Prawns,' said Fiona.

Typical, I thought. The very treat she had used to lure Jaffa away from me!

Bex chipped in: 'Great idea, Fiona. I know my Sparky would need to be dragged away snarling and biting if anyone tried to get between him and a plate of prawns.'

Dad looked at one of the takeaway dishes. 'Would prawn biryani work?' he asked doubtfully.

'Perfect,' said Bex.

'Hold on a minute,' I cut in, waving my hands to get their attention. 'Could someone please explain why we want to give a tasty treat to this horrible creature who has been bullying my Jaffsie?'

'We want to get a good long look at whatever it is, don't we?' said Nev. 'If you leave it something tasty to eat, it'll stay still long enough for us to get lots of lovely images of it. Then you can find out what it is you're dealing with. If it's a fox, say, then you know you've probably got to keep Jaffa in for a few days while you lure the fox out of your garden. You could tempt it away from the house by leaving food by the back fence so it doesn't need to come in and take Jaffa's,' he explained.

Nev certainly sounded as though he knew

what he was talking about, and for the first time in ages I felt reassured. I went to get some food and enjoy a nice normal evening with my friends while Nev laid the bait . . .

Well, at least the meal went without a hitch. Jazz was on sparkling form, chatting away to Fiona about the programme she was currently producing, and Dad and Bex seemed to have a lot to talk to Nev about. So that left me and Fergus. He offered to clear the plates and I grabbed the opportunity of a quiet word with him, jumping up to gather the empty foil dishes.

We took everything over to the sink.

'Awesome party!' Fergus joked, nodding at the noisy group around the table. 'Good to see Jazz on form too.'

'Yeah, I've been meaning to ask you – about the audition. You sure you didn't know anything about it?' I pressed, keeping my voice low so that

Jazz wouldn't hear me.

Fergus shook his head. 'I already told you, there were no auditions for anything yesterday. The hall was closed. We weren't even allowed to have band practice. The teachers wanted to chuck us out on time cos it was Friday. Anyway, I've been with Kezia loads this week and she never said anything about putting on a show or holding auditions, and she would have said something to Rashid, wouldn't she? He's been involved in all the discos and shows and stuff for the past two years.'

I flicked my eyes in Jazz's direction and saw she was staring at me, mouthing, 'What?'

'OK,' I said quickly to Fergus. 'We can't talk about this now. I'll call you tomorrow—'

CRASH!

A commotion in the utility room made us all jump out of our skins. Jazz screamed, and a plate slipped from my soapy fingers and smashed on the floor.

'What the . . . ?' Dad flung his chair back and whizzed over to the door.

Nev nipped in front of Dad and barred the way. 'We could have a situation in there,' he said dramatically. He nodded in the direction of the laptop which lay forgotten on the kitchen work surface.

On the screen there was a very clear close-up of the back end of the intruder enjoying its prawn curry with relish. It was guzzling the food without stopping, one hundred and ten per cent focused on what it was doing.

'It's huge!' breathed Jazz, her eyes wide in amazement.

'What is it?' Dad said, horrified.

'Impossible to tell from this angle,' said Nev.

All we could see was a large furry bottom filling the screen. It looked as though the animal was black and white, or possibly grey and white, but as the camera had been set on night vision, so there was no colour, we couldn't be sure.

'Could it . . . It couldn't be a badger, could it?' I whispered. Poor Jaffsie! No wonder she had been terrified.

'Only one thing for it,' said Nev. He pulled back his shoulders and, locking his hands, stretched them away from his body, making the knuckles crack. 'I'm going in.'

15

Intruder Apprehended

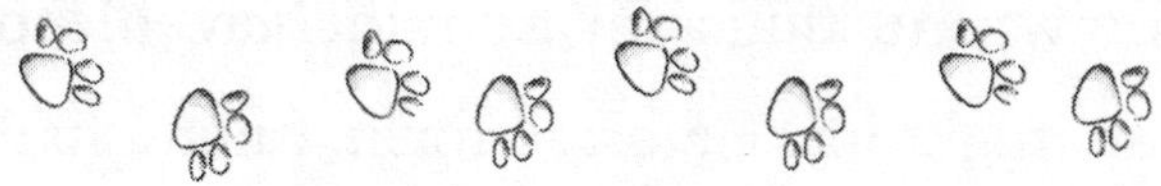

'Go for it, Nev,' said Dad, a steely glint in his eye.

'What?' I stammered.

Nev was rubbing his hands together and asking for a large towel.

'Wouldn't some gardening gloves, or even oven gloves, be better?' Bex asked nervously. 'What if it scratches you?' She was biting her nails, her brow furrowed. 'I mean, we know that this is a pretty vicious creature, don't we, Bertie?'

I nodded dumbly.

'Bertie and I have seen the kind of chaos this animal can cause, you see, Nev . . .' Bex was babbling a bit now.

'Yes, well, so have I,' said Dad grimly. 'And now it's payback time. Go on, Nev!' he urged. 'What are you waiting for?'

Jazz was backing away from the screen, looking as if she might make a break for it. I put a hand on her arm. 'It's OK,' I whispered. 'There's only one of it and seven of us.'

She twisted her mouth and frowned, but stood still, keeping her eyes fixed firmly on the screen.

Meanwhile, Nev had grabbed the big towel we keep on the back of the kitchen door to dry our hands. He tiptoed soundlessly to the utility-room door, opened it very slowly and completely silently, and then—

'He's got it!' Fiona gasped hoarsely, pointing at the wriggling, writhing towel on the screen.

Nev had pounced and was now holding the creature down, grimacing as he fought to stop it escaping.

After a couple of seconds he appeared to get

the bundle under control and swiftly tucked it under his arm.

He came back into the kitchen, laughing nervously and sweating slightly.

'Jazz was right, it *is* huge!' he exclaimed. 'And it sure knows how to put up a struggle.'

It certainly did. The towel was bobbing up and down like an overexcited Halloween ghost.

'Eeeeeeeeeeeeaaaaaoooooow!'

Blimey, it even *sounded* like a ghost . . .

'Quick!' Fergus ordered, watching as the bundle struggled even more. 'Secure all exits and entrances!'

I darted to the door into the hall and slammed it, relieved that Jaffa was upstairs out of harm's way. Bex leaped to close the utility-room door. Everyone else stood around Nev in a circle, waiting for the great unveiling.

'Ready to release the suspect?' asked Nev.

'I s'pose so,' said Bex quietly.

'Oh, I can't look!' Jazz squeaked.

'Come on!' Dad said impatiently. 'One, two, three!'

Nev whisked the blanket away.

We all gasped in unison.

There on the floor in front of us, crouched in a quivering, huddled bundle, looking up at us with big green eyes and a particularly sorry-for-itself expression on its smudgy grey and white features, was a cat. A large cat, it's true. But a cat all the same. An ordinary old moggie. Somebody's pet.

'No . . . !' breathed Bex. Her eyes were out on stalks.

I had a feeling she was thinking what I was thinking: boy, had we been fooled! I didn't

know whether to laugh or to run from the room to find my kitten and give her a good talking-to. She had *so* dropped me in it! I was mortified! All this hassle over a cat! Why hadn't she *said* so? I could *talk* to cats, for heaven's sake; I could have sorted out this bullying business days ago.

'Oh, man,' Fergus said in hushed tones. 'All that fuss and bother just for a big old fluffy bundle like that!'

The cat seemed to frown and let out a low menacing growl. 'Less of the "big" and "old", mate,' it sneered.

I jumped.

'Err, Fergus,' I stammered, 'I – er . . . I don't think he likes you saying that about him.'

'Too right I don't, missy,' the cat snarled.

Fergus was looking at me with a distinctly worried expression, but luckily for me, we were both distracted by an even stranger sound than the growling.

'Awwwwww!'

I whipped round to where the sound was coming from.

'Look at the poor lickle puddy tat!'

'Jazz . . . ?'

My best mate's face had crumpled. Her eyes were wide in sorrow and her eyebrows knitted together in a worried frown. Her hands were clasped to her chest and she was making very peculiar whimpering noises. I wondered for a moment if she was in pain.

'Are you feeling all right, Jazz?' Fergus asked, laying a hand on her shoulder.

'You do look a bit wobbly,' Bex added. 'Do you want a glass of water?'

But Jazz seemed not to hear what was being said. In fact she didn't seem to hear or, come to that, *see* anyone other than the scruffy, scowling grey and white cat who was huffing and puffing on the floor in front of her.

Dad was peering at the cat too. He rubbed at his chin and then said, 'Do you know, I think I recognize him.' He scratched his head. 'I'd swear it's the Morrises' moggie, but they moved away weeks ago. Did you meet them, Fiona?'

'I'm certainly glad we've blocked up the cat flap at our place,' said Fiona sniffily, rudely ignoring Dad. 'Nasty brute.'

That was nice, I thought, coming from the woman who had once told me how much she 'simply *adored* cats'.

'Oh dear,' said Bex. 'So you think he's a stray, Nigel?'

'I don't know,' Dad said, shooting an annoyed glance in Fiona's direction, 'but if it is their cat, he must be homeless. The Morrises have gone – I saw the removal vans. The house has been empty ever since.'

'Don't I know it,' said the cat gruffly. 'I've tried all the other 'ouses in the neighbour'ood, but yours is the only one what'll let a poor cat in. Until recently, that is. I even tried getting into Mrs Nose-in-the-air's 'ouse,' he added, narrowing his eyes at Fiona. 'But I couldn't get in, seeing how as yer'd *blocked your flippin' cat flap as well.*' I chewed my lip. If only she could hear what he was saying! He went on: 'So I 'ad to do something, didn't I? I've been starvin', not to mention cold and lonely. Those Morris numbskulls were all over me one minute, feeding me, giving me cuddles, letting me sleep on their beds; the next minute they were gone.'

I felt a pang at his words. He might have bullied my Jaffa, but no cat should be left to fend for itself like that.

'So *that's* why you—' I stopped myself – in time, I hoped. I had started speaking before I had realized what I was doing: 'I mean that's why *he's* been sneaking into our house to steal food. Well, it makes sense, doesn't it?' I babbled, catching a concerned glance from Fergus, who was evidently

wondering if I had lost every last marble in the pack. 'If the family who owns him has moved and left him behind, he'll have been hungry and lonely and that's why he's been breaking in and taking Jaffa's food,' I added, 'translating' what the cat had said to me.

'Poor thing,' said Bex, shaking her head.

'Oh, the darling little kitty-cat!' Jazz whispered, staring at the cat, her face creased in pity.

It was one thing to hear Bex voice concern for the abandoned cat – she was a pet-shop owner and an animal-lover like me, after all. But *Jazz*? I gawped in disbelief at my friend, expecting her to break into a raucous cackle of laughter and flap her hands at me as if it was all one huge, hilarious joke.

But instead she just shook her head sadly and said hoarsely, 'How could anyone abandon him like that? He must be so lonely.' She was now gazing at the cat as though he was the most beautiful sight she had ever had the good fortune to behold.

Dad snorted quietly, but quickly coughed to cover it up when he too realized that this was not a laughing matter. For now the cat was suddenly looking rather weird. His green eyes, which had been so mean and steely, were now wide and shining, and he was staring back at Jazz with an expression of deep devotion.

It was Fergus who broke the silence. 'Wow. This is freaky. It looks like a case of love at first sight!' he said light-heartedly.

But the thing was, I had a creeping suspicion that this was no joke at all.

16

Love at First Sight

'Jazz – JAZZ!' I yelled at her and waved my arms madly in front of her face. It was as though she'd been hypnotized.

She jumped when she eventually focused on me and gave a little squeal. 'Hey! Stop that!'

'Is that it then?' Dad was saying, still sizing up the cat with a rather disgusted expression on his face. 'I mean, are you telling me that *this* is our mystery intruder? How in heaven's name does a common old moggie manage to create the havoc we've had to put up with recently? He doesn't look nearly big and ugly enough.'

Fergus shrugged and said through a cheeky

grin, 'Well, you'd hardly call him *minuscule* and *adorable*, would you?'

'Oi, watch it, buster,' the cat said rudely.

I swallowed nervously. I hoped he wasn't about to kick off again.

'Hey, you.'

I stared at the cat.

'Yeah, you. The one with the frizzy hair and the stupid look on her face.'

Great. So he was insulting me. And I couldn't answer back.

I gave as slight a nod of the head as I could manage in the hope that the humans in the room would not notice.

'You gonna let me outta this hellhole, or what?' the cat growled.

I shook my head.

Fergus let out a whoosh of breath and tapped his foot impatiently. 'Are we just going to stand here and stare at this monster, or are we going to

give him a good soaking and send him packing?' he said.

'NO!' Jazz shrieked, turning on Fergus, total and utter outrage etched across her face. She seemed to have rediscovered her voice at last. 'How can you be so MEAN? Look at the fluffy little darling! He wouldn't hurt a flea, would you, pusskins?' And, to our amazement, she bent down and scooped the ginormous bundle into her arms and started crooning to him as though he was a newborn baby.

Fiona tutted and said, 'Come on, Fergie. I think it's time to go. Are you all right to pack up here, Nev? Nigel, darling, it's been an, er, interesting evening . . .'

Nev was scratching his head. 'Yeah, I'll go and get my kit and head off, if that's all right with you guys.' He backed out of the room and started dismantling his camera equipment.

'Bertie?' Fergus said, looking at me. 'Can I stay for a bit?'

'Whatever,' I said. I wanted them all to leave. I wanted to go upstairs right away and confront Jaffa about her so-called tormentor. Or did I? It wasn't her fault, and she really had been scared. In her eyes the cat was still a monster. Thinking of that made me want to console her and cuddle her and tell her it was all over and she was safe now.

Bex and Dad showed Fiona and Nev out. While they were saying their goodbyes, Jazz carried on talking the biggest load of nonsense I had ever heard from her in all the long years she had been my mate.

'Awww, you are the softest, most scrumptious-est, delumptiousest sweetie-pie catkins dat I have ever *seeeeeen*!' she squawked.

The cat broke out into the loudest fit of purring *I* had ever *heard*. 'And you are the most gorgeous girl I've ever seen, babe,' he crooned.

My pity for the animal quickly turned to disgust. Oh please fetch a bucket, someone, I thought,

pulling a puking face at Fergus.

But of course he hadn't heard what the cat had said. And he was so baffled by Jazz's behaviour that he was just staring, dumbfounded, at the lovebirds (or should that be love-*cats*?), at a complete loss for words.

'I saw yer,' the cat to me. 'Pulling that face. Just shut it, mate, or I'll shut it for yer, all right?'

I clenched my fists and narrowed my eyes. Poor homeless cat he might be, but he was *not* going to get away with talking to me like that. My blood was boiling, and without thinking I said, 'Watch it yourself, mate.'

'What?' said Fergus.

'That cat!' I blurted out, torn between giving the moggie a piece of my mind and preserving my dignity. 'I know I should probably feel sorry for him, but . . . but . . . he terrorizes my little cat and causes havoc in my house for days and days, and then when he's caught red-handed, all he can do is snuggle up to Jazz and make eyes at her as if nothing's happened! The cheek of it—'

'Grrrr!' the cat growled.

'Oh, shh, Bertie!' Jazz simpered, frowning at me. 'You've gone and upset the little pusskins now.'

'Bertie . . .' said Fergus, looking anxiously from me to Jazz. He was backing away from us slightly as if *we* were two unpredictable wild animals. 'I, er, I should point out that this is a *cat* we're talking about. Moggies don't think things through in the way you're suggesting. I think—'

'You don't think at all, buster,' hissed the cat. 'And for your information, I am not a *moggie*. The name's Bob.'

'BOB?' I spat in disbelief. 'What kind of a name is that for a cat?'

'No way am I calling him that!' cried Jazz. 'This little baby's going to be called Cupid from now on. And *I'm* going to take care of him,' she added decisively.

'CUPID?' I was shouting now. Had the whole world gone mad?

'Yes,' said Jazz primly. 'Because he's stolen my heart.'

'Cupid? CUPID? *STUPID,* MORE LIKE!' I yelled, stamping my foot in anger.

Jazz shot me a look of utter outrage. 'How can you be so mean to the poor little puss-cat?'

'Er, you two—' Fergus tried stepping in between us, but then Bob-Stupid-Cupid started kicking off.

'You shut it right now!' he warned me again in a low growl that was gaining in volume every second. 'If this gorgeous babe wants to look after me and give me a new name, that's her lookout,' he said. 'Happens to us cats all the time. I couldn't give a haddock's armpit what I'm called.' And he rubbed his head against Jazz and purred so loudly it sounded like a swarm of dragonflies had invaded the room.

'There, see?' said Jazz with satisfaction. 'He likes his name! The lickle-ickle sweetheart . . .'

Dad came back in at this point and made an announcement. 'Bex has gone too. She had to see to Sparky. And, guys,' he added firmly, 'it's getting late. We need to decide what to do with this beast.'

Bob-Cupid growled at Dad, flattening his ears and baring his teeth threateningly.

Dad took a step back and said, 'Bex reckoned we should call the Cats and Dogs Home and take him there, but if you ask me –' he glanced at his watch and yawned – 'I think we should chuck the rascal out, tape up the cat flap with duct tape and go to bed. Fergus, if you want to stay you can have the camp bed in my study. Jazz, if you still want to stay, you can sleep on the pull-out mattress in Bertie's room like you normally do. We'll clear up the rest of the dishes in the morning.'

He stood and looked expectantly at us all.

'Well?' he said.

No one moved.

Cupid – Bob – whatever his name was – wriggled in Jazz's arms. 'No one's chucking me out!' he spat. 'I'll go quietly, thanks. I know when I'm not wanted.'

I felt a pang in my chest, in spite of my anger. I couldn't let Dad chuck him out. It was being abandoned in the first place that had caused all the trouble. I was going to say so to Dad, but Jazz got there first.

'Hey! You are not going anywhere, my little darling!' she said to the wriggling bundle in her arms.

Boy, I wished she would stop all this lovey-dovey rubbish.

The cat stopped struggling and sneered at me defiantly.

I raised my eyebrows. 'I'm not the one who suggested chucking you out,' I hissed.

Dad sighed loudly and said, 'You know what? I

can't deal with this right now. As long as there are no more noises and no more breakages, I think I'm just going to go to bed and we'll sort this out in the morning. Jazz, take the cat home with you if you're so worried about him. Do whatever you like, but just go and get some kip. All of you.' He turned his back on us before we could protest.

I sighed noisily, but I had to agree with Dad. It was pretty clear we were not going to get a word of sense out of Jazz now that it seemed like a spaceshipful of aliens had drilled a hole in her head and sucked all the brains out.

'Come on, Fergus,' I said wearily. 'I'll help you set up the camp bed. Stay down here for a minute, hey, Jazz? I'll come back down once I've made sure Jaffa's safely back in my room. I don't want her seeing Bo— I mean Cupid. OK?' I peered at Jazz.

But she hadn't heard a word I'd said: her face was buried in Cupid's tummy and she was making squeaking noises and giggling, while the cat purred

so loudly it sounded like he was going to take off. I rolled my eyes and left the pair of them to it.

Fergus and I went up to Dad's study. We went in quietly and saw Jaffa asleep on Dad's papers, where I had left her. How she had not heard any of the goings-on downstairs I did not know. She looked so adorable, her eyes tight shut, her face half hidden by her skinny tail, her body rising and falling with each tiny snuffly snore.

'How could that horrible cat hurt you?' I whispered.

'What are you going to do with her tonight?' Fergus asked as we wrestled with the frame of the camp bed, trying to get it out of Dad's cupboard without knocking the rest of the contents out on to the floor. 'Do you want me to look after her in here?'

'No! She's sleeping on my bed tonight. If Jazz is so loved-up, she can take Stupid Cupid back to her place,' I hissed. 'There's no way I'm giving him the chance of scaring Jaffsie again.'

'OK. Don't get stressy,' Fergus teased.

I stuck my tongue out at him.

He did the same to me and then paused in thought. 'I don't get it, you know,' he said. 'I thought Jazz didn't even *like* cats.'

'She doesn't.' I puffed out my cheeks and blew at my fringe, which was sticking to my forehead. I gave the bed frame one last tug and finally freed it from a bunch of wire coat hangers and a collection of empty shoeboxes. I made a mental note to remind Dad of the state of that cupboard the next time he had a go at me to tidy my room.

'Careful!' Fergus squeaked, staggering back against Dad's desk as he took the brunt of the frame. He glanced around anxiously. 'Don't think your dad would be too impressed if I knocked his scripts all over the floor.'

Jaffa lifted her head sleepily and said, 'What is the Fergus doing, bumpin' into things and

making a rumpus-noise?'

'Shhh, don't worry,' I said, reaching across and stroking her small head. 'Go back to sleep.' I didn't want to tell her about Cupid just then. Not until he was safely out of the house.

Jaffa settled back snugly on to the paper pile. Dad's desk was in a worse state than his cupboard, I noticed. I knew he was in the middle of a new play, but it looked more like he was in the middle of fifty-six new plays, if the amount of paper on his desk was anything to go by.

'Yeah, well, he should be more *tidy*, shouldn't he?' I said in response to Fergus, with a glint in my eye. 'Listen, what are we going to do about Jazz? It's like she's been brainwashed by a weird religious cult or something. Do you think she's going to try to keep Bob – I mean, Cupid?'

Fergus narrowed his eyes. 'Why do you keep calling him Bob?'

I blushed and looked away. 'I . . . I dunno. He

just looks like a Bob. There was this guy at my old school called Bob, and he looks a bit like him. He was a big bruiser too!' I gave a fake laugh. 'Anyway, you've got to admit Bob suits him better than Cupid.'

Fergus spluttered with laughter. 'Yeah! Actually, almost any name would suit him better than that!'

I said goodnight to Fergus and was still sniggering as I tiptoed along the landing to my room with Jaffa in my arms. But my laughter didn't last long.

The minute I opened the door, Jaffa went ballistic. She jammed her claws into my arms and her fur stuck up, making her look like a furry orange porcupine. I yowled at her to let go of me, and was so busy wrestling to calm her down that I didn't see right away what she was squealing about.

'Bertie! Bertie!' she shrieked. 'Jazzer got the nasty Mr Bob-Cat who been a big old bully to Jaffsie! He say I must not tell on him or he really,

really goin' to hurt me! Jazzer got the nasty Mr Bob-Cat! Bertie get the nasty cat away from Jaffsie!'

That was when I took a proper look at the scene before me. Jazz was sitting on my bed clutching a hissing, spitting Cupid while hysterically whispering at him to, 'Shhhh!' and, 'Quieten down and do what Mumsie tells you,' and threatening, 'If you don't be a good boy, we won't be able to stay here.'

I quickly pulled the door shut behind me while holding on tight to Jaffa. She was desperate to escape, but there was no way I was going to let her. Immediately she proved quite how desperate she was by giving me a sharp nip, forcing me to drop her, at which point she zoomed up on top of the curtain rail, as far away from Jazz and her enemy as was possible. She was screeching with fright, mewling and whining like I had never heard before. She hadn't been this upset even when we took her to the vet for her vaccinations.

'Jazz!' I yelled, opening the door to my room again. 'What are you *doing*, bringing that cat up here? I told you I didn't want to scare Jaffa. She's gone mental!' I turned to the cats and called out, 'You've got to quieten down – both of you!' I paid particular attention to Cupid as I said this.

'Why are you looking at Cupid like that?' Jazz asked suspiciously. 'It's your kitten that's making all the noise.'

'Just shut up and hold on to that . . . that *animal* while I try to calm Jaffa down,' I ordered.

Jazz glared at me. 'I thought you *loved* animals, Bertie. Just because Cupid has been a naughty boy, there is no need to be nasty to him. He needs love and attention just as much as Jaffa. And I am not letting him out of my sight. We need to be together.'

'OK, so how do you suggest we organize things tonight then?' I said bitterly, keeping one eye on Jaffa and one on Cupid. Maybe I'd go so cross-eyed my eyeballs would explode, I thought angrily.

That would add a nice dimension to the night. 'I am NOT having that BULLY in my room. And I don't think your mum would take kindly to you turning up in the middle of the night with a stray moggie under your arm,' I added pointedly.

'Will yer stop calling me that?' Bob growled.

'Well, what should I call you then?' I shouted, forgetting myself in my anger.

Jazz didn't notice though. She was too busy shaking her head and curling her lip at me in disdain. 'You know what?' she said. 'I don't think Cupid and I *want* to share a room with you when you're in this kind of mood anyway. I'll kip on the sofa. Cupid can keep me warm, can't you, my little squidgy-kins?'

I let out a whoosh of air and threw my head back in exasperation. 'ANYTHING,' I roared, 'for a bit of peace and quiet and sanity around here.'

17

New Home Sweet Home?

The next morning I found Fergus in the kitchen, clearing up the remains of the meal from the night before. He had swept up the fragments from the broken plate and had even put the kettle on and laid the table for breakfast.

'Least I could do.' He smiled bashfully. 'I couldn't help thinking you might like a hand. And I'm not sure you're going to get any help from Jazz. She just stormed out into the garden, after I tried to explain that she would have to let us find a home for the cat.'

'What?' I mumbled blearily. My brain was not fully in gear yet after the disrupted night I'd had.

Even once Jazz and Bob-Cupid had finally gone downstairs, my poor traumatized kitten had refused to come down from the curtain pole and it had taken a lot of persuading to stop her hysterical mewling. I was bushed. I rubbed my eyes and ran a hand through my hair.

Fergus leaned the broom he was using against the edge of the table and grabbed the dustpan and brush. As he knelt to gather the small pile of rubbish he'd swept up he said, 'The thing is, I know your dad *thought* the cat belonged to a family who'd moved away, but I was thinking that we should at least put up posters or something. Just in case. I mean . . .' He hesitated. 'I remember how upset *you* were when Mum took Jaffa in, thinking she was a stray.' He looked up at me.

I let slip a small smile. Of course, *I* knew that Dad's presumption had been correct, because Bob – sorry, *Cupid* – had said as much himself. He had been abandoned by his owners. I just wasn't sure I wanted his new owner to be my best friend. For a start it would mean he would be living a bit too close for comfort. What if he took it into his head to keep on coming round to terrorize Jaffa whenever he felt like it?

I decided to play along with the poster idea.

'Yeah, you're right. We probably should make some posters.' I yawned and stretched. 'Give me that.' I gestured to the dustpan full of grot. 'I'll get rid of it and you make some tea. When Dad gets down we can hatch a plan.'

'What's this? Not another plan?' Dad had emerged, looking as rough as I felt: his hair sticking up in freaky clumps and his eyes baggy with lack of sleep. He was cleaning his glasses on the edge of his pyjama top and blinking like a tortoise coming out of hibernation.

Fergus busied himself with the mugs and tea bags, probably embarrassed at the sight of Dad in his PJs. I cringed – couldn't he at least have pulled

on jeans and a T-shirt? 'Er, yeah, we were just talking about finding out who B— the cat's real owners were,' I said. Go and get dressed! I shouted at him in my head.

Dad peered at me and then put his glasses on. 'Ah, that's better,' he said. 'I can see who I'm talking to now . . . Blimey, Bertie, you look a sight!'

'Huh!' I retorted. 'You can talk.'

'Would you like a cup of tea?' Fergus said, a bit too loudly.

Dad's face changed abruptly from miffed-with-his-daughter to chuffed-with-his-guest. 'That would be lovely, Fergus,' he beamed, managing nevertheless to shoot me a narrow-eyed look at the same time. He pulled back a chair and plonked himself down, yawning again.

'So,' I said, carefully taking a mug of tea from Fergus. 'Are you sure that cat belongs to the Morrises?'

Dad shrugged, gulping his scalding tea. His

glasses steamed up. He swallowed painfully and then said in a rasping voice, 'Not one hundred per cent sure.'

'Fergus thinks we *need* to be certain,' I said.

'It would be awful if we found him a new home while all the time there was a family out there missing him like crazy,' Fergus added.

He immediately looked sheepish as Dad raised his eyebrows and piped up in a teasing tone, 'Would it? Would it really? OK,' he said, suddenly serious again. 'I'll ask Bex to help out. She can put up posters in her shop and around town, and we can do our bit in the neighbourhood. Now . . .'

He jumped up and went to rummage in the drawer where we keep odd scraps of paper and a jumble of pens and pencils. He pulled out pen after pen, scribbling on some paper until he found one that worked. 'Really must sort this drawer out,' he muttered. Finally he came back to the table with a pink ballpoint pen resplendent with a flashing

fairy on the top. I rolled my eyes.

'So, what should we say?' Dad asked, looking from Fergus to me.

Fergus chewed his bottom lip and then said, in a tight voice that was clearly bursting with barely held-back laughter, 'Erm . . . "Cat found. If you don't want it, we know a girl who does"? That's Jazz, I mean,' he added hastily, catching the horrified look on my face.

Dad frowned. 'I think we'll have to do a bit better than that. Bertie?'

'How about "Aggressive, deranged beast found terrorizing beloved family pet – come and get it now before we take it to the Cats and Dogs Home"?'

I had been expecting a curt telling-off from Dad about my Tone of Voice, but instead his eyes lit up. 'Cats and Dogs Home!' he exclaimed. 'Of course! That's what Bex suggested last night.' He glanced at the kitchen clock. 'I'll give them a call and tell them we've found a cat. They don't need to know the gory details. Meanwhile, you two can figure out the poster.'

He went to find the phone book while Fergus and I argued over the wording. We were so deep in discussion that we didn't see Jazz come in from the garden with Cupid in her arms.

'What are you doing?' she snapped.

I whirled round guiltily. 'Nothing!' I lied.

Fergus looked up at Jazz from under his floppy fringe. 'Well – we are doing something, obviously,' he burbled. 'Just nothing that you need to, er, get involved with.'

Jazz made a good attempt at giving us one of her you-two-are-complete-numpties looks while juggling with the wriggling and obviously pretty heavy cat.

'Tell the babe to put me down a minute, can't you?' Cupid growled at me. 'I need to pay a quick visit to the flower beds, if you get my meaning.'

'Now, Fluffykins,' Jazz gushed, 'why is my baby being such a wriggle-puss? Oh, *what* is the matter, Mr Snuggly?'

I coughed. 'I think 'Mr Snuggly' needs a little wee-wee.'

Not that I was keen on him digging up half the garden. He was such a massive meathead of a cat, I was sure he wouldn't be discreet about where he chose to do his business, and if he trashed the garden Dad would freak. But I couldn't say any of that to him without Jazz and Fergus thinking I'd gone fruit-loop-bananas crazy. I chose to give Cupid a good hard 'Paddington stare' instead, hoping that would convey my feelings.

Cupid seemed to get the message. 'Don't lose your rag, girl,' he snarled. 'I'll tidy up after. I'm not an untamed beast.'

'Riiiiight!' I muttered sarcastically.

'OH!' cried Jazz, finally reacting to what I had said. 'Of *course* he needs a wee!' She picked him up

again and looked wildly around the room. 'And, er, where should I take him?' she asked helplessly.

'I would probably try outside, like where you've just *been*,' I said to the ceiling.

'And make it snappy or I'll 'ave an accident,' said Cupid.

While he was doing his business outside, Jazz turned to me, all misty-eyed, and said, 'I'm going to take him home and ask Mum if I can keep him.'

I felt a cold sensation grip my insides.

At that moment Dad came in. 'Well, I called them and they said they hadn't had any calls regarding a large male cat.'

'You called who exactly?' Jazz said, her voice icy with suspicion.

Dad faltered. 'The . . . the Cats and Dogs Home. You told Jazz, right?' he said, looking at me with a worried frown.

'Haven't had a chance,' I muttered.

'THE CATS AND DOGS HOME?' Jazz yelled,

hands on hips, chin jutting forward in outrage.

Dad put out one hand in a calming gesture, as if holding back a wild beast.

'Now Jazz, don't overreact. You must see that we have to try to find the cat's owners.'

Cupid came crashing back in to see Jazz in full throttle, gesticulating and arguing with Dad and pleading with me and Fergus not to make the posters.

'What 'ave you said to 'er?' Cupid demanded, baring his teeth at me, his fur bristling.

I took advantage of the mayhem and bent down to talk to this brute of an animal. 'Now you listen to me,' I hissed at him. 'I haven't said anything. This is all your fault. First you come uninvited into my home, trash the place and bully my kitten, and now you've got your claws well and truly into my best mate. If I were you, I'd make a break for it while no one's looking and find your way back home. Now.'

Cupid hissed back at me. 'You don't get it, do you, Frizz-ball?' he said menacingly. 'I told you already – I ain't got *no home to go to*. The guy with the glasses and the mad 'air was right. It was the Morrises what used to feed me and that. And now they've gone. Vamoosh. Fade to grey – got it? They disappeared without so much as a 'see you around' and left me to fend for myself. Typical flippin' humans, if you ask me. You're all the same, just out for your own interests. Except my beautiful babe there.' He ran over to Jazz, turning on the motorized purring, and wound his way in and out of her legs. 'This one's different. She knows what a cat needs.'

I was boiling with fury. Jazz knew nothing about cats! And this cat knew nothing about Jazz.

'Well,' I said, through gritted teeth, 'you're not going to be hanging around long enough to find out just how much she does or doesn't know, *mate*, cos if we find out it's true and the Morrises really have left you, that makes you a stray, so we're tak-

ing you to the Cats and Dogs Home. Now, do *you* "get it"?'

Cupid arched his back and bared his fangs at me like an angry snake. But I was not going to let this bully intimidate me in the same way he had Jaffa.

'Bertie! What have you done to poor Mr Squidgy Pusskins?' Jazz swung the horrible cat up into her arms, where he immediately turned into a purring fluffy cuddly ball once more.

'I thought you said his name was Cupid,' I mumbled, folding my arms in annoyance. 'If you can't even make up your mind what you're going to call him, I hardly think you're the right person to give him a new home.'

Fergus was shaking his head. 'And anyway, how do you think your mum will feel if you come back from a sleepover with a huge fat cat in your arms and announce he's going to live with you?'

Jazz abruptly stopped her cooing and billing over Cupid-Mr-Squidgy-Fluffykins and looked at us, her features suddenly frozen with anxiety. 'I hadn't thought about that!' she croaked. 'Oh, my gorgeous kitty-cat – what am I going to do if I can't keep you?'

'Don't listen to them, darlin'. You'll think of something,' Cupid assured her.

Jazz hesitated and was about to set Cupid down on the floor, but instead a smile slowly crept across her face and she looked at me, a dangerous twinkle lighting up her chocolate-brown eyes. 'You know, Mum is more of a softie than you think. Remember how Tyson got her to let him have Huckleberry? If

I just take Cupid home with me now and tell Mum the whole sad story, I reckon there's no way she could bear to chuck him out,' she said craftily. 'And once Mum's made up her mind about something, there's no stopping her.'

'Like mother, like daughter,' I muttered. I couldn't help thinking Jazz was being more than a little bit optimistic.

'Sounds like a luverley family,' Cupid purred, stretching up to rub his head against Jazz's cheek.

Dad stepped in. 'You know, if you think she wouldn't mind you looking after him for a while, I have to say I think that's the best option. And he does seem very fond of you,' he added.

I glared at him.

'What?' he said, looking genuinely puzzled. 'Someone's got to look after him while we try to find out who his real owners are, and it seems a bit mean to take him straight to the Cats and Dogs Home if Jazz is set on caring for him.'

I curled my lip and was about to launch into a tirade about how mean Cupid had been to Jaffa and how if Dad thought I was going to tolerate him living on the same street as us then—

But Fergus cut in with, 'Great idea. Come on, Bertie, you have to admit it's the best plan. You can't look after the cat yourself because of how he's upset Jaffa. And the Cats and Dogs Home is a bit, well, grim.'

I laughed. 'I don't WANT to look after him, thanks very much. And as for grim—'

'Right, that's settled then,' said Dad decisively. 'I'll come back with you, Jazz, and help explain to your mum if you like.'

'Yes, please,' said Jazz, shooting me a triumphant glance.

So the cat who'd been bullying my kitten was getting preferential treatment, and I got no say in things at all.

Thanks a lot, guys.

18
Undercover Agent

The next day was Monday, and Jazz had texted me and Fergus before we got to the bus.

V impt + xtra urgnt stff 2 tell U!!!!! ☺

When I saw her at the bus stop and asked her what was up, she kept putting her finger to her lips and shushing me, looking around nervously. Fergus saw us huddled together and waved over the top of the other kids' heads. He came to join us. 'So what's the big deal?' he said.

'Nothing!' said Jazz irritably.

'OK,' he said, rolling his eyes at me. 'No need to get . . .'

'*Stressy!*' we said together, laughing and jabbing Jazz in the ribs.

Jazz scowled. 'I'll tell you in a minute,' she said. 'Just shut up till we're on the bus, can't you?'

We filed on and found some seats in a row. Fergus leaned towards us, his fringe falling across his face, and said, 'Come on then, Jazz. Spill the beans.'

'Shhhh!' she said noisily. 'Someone might hear you!' She looked around wildly as though we were being spied on.

'Er, I don't think so,' I said pointedly, nodding my head in the direction of the fight that had already broken out at the back between a crowd of Year 8 boys. Anyone else was either getting involved or firmly plugging earphones in so that they didn't have to hear the racket.

Jazz slumped back into her seat and slid down to make herself as small as possible. 'OK,' she said quietly, 'but you'll have to lean in so I can whisper – I don't want Charlie and Kezia to hear this.'

Wasn't I the lucky one, being told something that the Gruesome Twosome weren't supposed to know!

'Go on,' I said, hunkering down. Fergus craned his neck further so he could hear too.

'It's this totally wicked thing – it's just awesome, you won't believe it!' she whispered, her voice ending in a squeak. 'I was Googling stuff about cats – you know, what they like to eat, where they like to sleep, what treats they like, what to do to settle a cat in a new—'

'Yeah, yeah,' I cut in impatiently, 'I know the stuff you mean. And?'

'Well, it's, like, so amazingly cool, you have no idea – there is this programme, right, called *Cat's Eye*, in the States, yeah? And what they do is they get these cats and they put them in a special kind of hotel for cats. They give them mega-comfy beds and bowls of treats and they put them in lovely collars and let them have funky cat toys and that, and then they film them! It's like *Big Brother*, but for *cats*! Immense or what?'

She looked at me, her mouth and eyes wide open as if she'd just told me the most earth-shattering piece of information I was ever likely to hear in my entire life. Fergus caught my eye and curled his lip in a she's-really-lost-it-this-time kind of way.

'Well?' Jazz said, her voice rising. So much for keeping it all hush-hush. 'Aren't you going to say anything?'

'I, er, like, wow?' I said, my forehead creasing in puzzlement.

'What are you going on about, Jazz?' asked Fergus.

'So, I reckon this is the most fabulous idea for a TV show *ever*, and I think we should make our own version. Don't you see? It would be the *best* sequel to *Pets with Talent*. We could film it at my house! I reckon Danni Minnow would love it. You

remember how much she adored Jaffa? Well, she's going to fall head over heels when she sees my gorgeous little fluffy-wuffy Mr Cupid. And you have absolutely *got* to see the clips I found on the Net. Once you've seen them, I know you'll agree with my plan.'

'Which is?' I asked nervously, a plummeting sick feeling swilling around in my stomach.

'Which is that I'm going to show the clips to Fiona and ask her if she thinks it's got legs,' said Jazz, putting on her know-it-all voice.

'What?' I exclaimed. 'What's *legs* got to do with it? Are you saying some of the cats on this programme don't have legs? That's just gross! That's like a freak show or something!'

Fergus spluttered with laughter. 'You numpty, Bertie!'

'Yeah, *duuuuuuh*!' said Jazz, wobbling her head at me as if to say, 'You really are the thickest brick in the wall.'

'It's an *expression*,' she said. 'Like, "Let's see if this plan has legs" means "Let's see if it'll work".'

I flushed. 'Right,' I mumbled. 'I knew that.'

'Course you did,' said Fergus, winking at me and setting me off into a full-scale blush of the hottest deepest red ever.

'Mmm,' said Jazz, narrowing her eyes at me.

I had to admit I had loved the whole *Pets with Talent* thing, and it would be kind of cool to do another show with animals . . . but something in the extreme nature of Jazz's enthusiasm was making me feel uneasy. Plus I wasn't exactly bowled over by the idea of working with Fiona again. I mean, she'd been great about catching Jaffa's tormentor and everything, but that was just one evening in my own home. The idea of getting involved in a whole new TV show from scratch was something completely different. I thought maybe we should change the subject slightly, so I said carelessly, 'Anyway, what does your mum think of Bob?'

'CUPID!' Jazz shouted. 'His name is Cupid. I will not have anyone call my lickle baby that awful big-bruiser name.'

'Yeah, Cupid. Sorry, I forgot,' I fibbed.

Fergus was really enjoying himself now, having a good old laugh at the pair of us.

Jazz didn't notice though. She was off on one about that revolting nightmare of a beast. 'Mum *lurrrrrves* him, of course! He is such a gorgeous lickle fluffball – so cuddly-wuddly and he purrs all the time. It makes me so cross to think of anyone abandoning him. No wonder my poor baby got all frightened and started doing naughty things like breaking into your place. He must have been so worried, being left all on his lonesome, and his tummy-wummy must have been so rumbly—'

'Er, Jazz,' I cut in, 'no offence and all that, but you sound a bit mental when you use that "babykins" voice.'

Jazz leaned forward to glare at me briefly and

then slumped back again, cooing, 'Ahh, well, I just can't help it. Anyway, now he's got me as his mummy, everything will be OK.'

I gave her a you're-doing-it-again look and she rolled her eyes. 'OK! OK! But listen, about my idea for the TV show. What do you think, Fergus? Do you reckon your mum will go for it?'

Fergus looked very uncomfortable. 'I don't know, Jazz. I mean, last time was a bit of a one-off. I don't think—'

Jazz's face set into a sullen pout. She crossed her arms tightly and sat back heavily again, staring at the seat in front of her.

'Oh, Jazz, don't be like that,' Fergus pleaded. 'Look, I'm sorry. What do I know? All I'm saying is, don't get your hopes up too high.'

'Hey, it does sound like a cool idea,' I said to Jazz, trying to make her feel better.

But all I got in response was a 'Humpf!' as she plugged herself into her iPod.

I caught Fergus's eye, but he just shrugged.

Jazz didn't say another word to us the whole way to school.

Later that day at school I got the first sign of the real reasons for Jazz's madder-than-a-mongoose behaviour. It was while I was in the loos. There had been no one in there to start with, but pretty soon after I went into a cubicle I heard the sound of the door opening followed by two voices I recognized only too well by now.

'She's soooo lame,' cackled Kezia.

'Yeah, all that rubbish about her new liddle puddytat,' sneered Charlie. 'I bet he doesn't exist either. What a loser.'

'Too right he doesn't exist!' screeched Kezia. 'It's all in her freaky imagination, just like all that stuff about "Oh, I'm *such* good friends with Danni Minnow, she sends me emails *all* the time. In fact, I'm going to call her up about this idea I've had for a show we could do together, and it's going to have my gorgeous liddle puddytat in it. He's going to be a staaaar",' she said in a sing-song voice that I realized with a shiver was supposed to be an imitation of my best mate.

'Yeah, it's totally sad,' spat Charlie. 'I mean, did you see that rubbish show *Pets with Talent*? Sooo *borrrrring*. And little Jazzie-meena wasn't even supposed to be in it – she was just jumping around in the background, desperate to get her face on camera. It was her mate Bernie, or whatever her name is, who won the contest with that cute— I mean, er, that kitten thing.'

'Jazz hasn't even got within twenty metres of Danni Minnow, has she?' said Kezia, her voice so laced with spite I wondered she didn't choke on her own poison.

'It was soooo hilarious faking those auditions on Friday!' Charlie chuckled.

'Yeah!' Kezia hooted. 'What *was* that outfit?

Looked like she'd got it from a jumble sale.'

'From a recycling bin, more like. That silver belt thing she was wearing – was it s'posed to be a skirt, d'you reckon? And those bits of string and stuff in her hair. Man! She looked like a scare-crow!'

'I know!' Kezia was obviously enjoying this. 'And I nearly *died* when she gave us all that heart-felt "This is totally my dream come true, I've always wanted to perform in a talent show" rubbish. Anyone would think she was actually on *Who's Got Talent?* instead of auditioning for a school production!'

'Which doesn't even exist!' Charlie added with a snort.

'Yeah! And when she pressed "play" on that kiddies' CD player thing and that totally *lame* music started up . . . oh man! She was like the *worst* of those losers in the earliest *WGT* auditions – you know, like those guys who come on with a parrot that plays the piano with its beak or whatever. No, actually make that, like, *two million times* worse.'

'And her face when we started laughing and told her it was all a set-up!' Charlie screeched.

Kezia was giggling so hard now she was having trouble getting her words out. 'Yeah!' she squeaked. 'Like, sooooo hilarious. I cannot believe she fell for the whole thing.'

'She really thinks she is something, doesn't she? As if!' Charlie guffawed. 'Hey, what'll we do next?'

I was frozen to the loo seat! No wonder Jazz had acted weird when I asked her about the auditions. And no wonder she was a nightmare on Saturday . . . Poor, poor Jazz! How could those girls be so mean when my best mate worshipped the ground they walked on? She must have been so freaked; I knew she'd been nervous enough about auditioning as it was. And now Jazz was probably planning this cat show just to impress them. It made me sick how they were manipulating her.

But what could I do? I felt like an undercover agent – with my knickers round my ankles, admittedly . . . I held my breath and willed every fibre of my body to stay as still as possible until I heard them leave.

Kezia suddenly erupted into an even louder cackle. 'Get this: I've just had the most *immense* idea. You know I nicked her phone the other day? Well, I made a note of her number. . .'

'Yeah?' said Charlie, hanging on every word of her horrible mate's stinking little plan.

'So let's text her pretending we are Danni and ask her to call back! I can pretend to be Danni when she calls and say that I've spoken to Fergus's mum about a great idea for a show and I want her to be in it. Imagine how worked up she'll get about that! She'll go round the whole school telling everyone, and then when she asks Fergus's mum about it, she'll look sooooo stupid!'

'Kez, you are a legend,' said Charlie. 'That'll

shut the little squirt up. Even her best mate will drop her once she finds out it's a load of rubbish. It'll be, like, yeah, IN YOUR FACE, JASMEENA BROWN!'

The two girls shrieked with nasty high-pitched laughter and I heard a slapping sound which must have been them high-fiving each other. Then I heard the door bang and their laughter faded as they disappeared.

Once I was sure the coast was clear, I crept out of the cubicle. I washed my hands and stared at my reflection in the mirror. What on earth could I do in the face of such evil scheming? I was just little old Bertie Fletcher, a new girl in Year 7 with hair like a poodle and a brain full of mush. I was no match for these two. Plus it was bizarre how they knew exactly how to get to Jazz: now that she had come up with her *Cat's Eye* idea, she would be sure to fall for Kezia calling her and pretending to be Danni. I'd never be able to convince her it was all

another set-up. Not until that fact became all too obvious.

And by then it would be too late.

19

The Plot Thickens

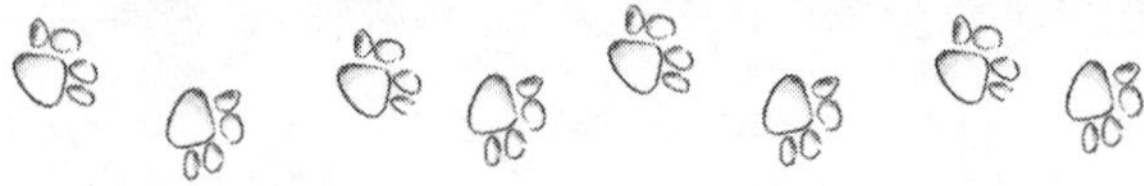

I spent the rest of that day worrying about Jazz. When I saw her at lunch, gossiping and laughing happily, it made me want to cry. To think that her life was maybe moments away from being made total hell by those horrible older girls. I felt panicky when I tried to work out what to do. Even if I told Fergus, what difference would it make? What if he laughed and said I must have misheard? Or worse, what if he got cross with me and blamed me for spreading false rumours?

I had almost convinced myself not to do anything by the time I queued up for the bus at the end of the day. I walked past Kezia and Charlie as I

looked for a free seat. They didn't notice me; they were too busy whispering behind their hideous neon-pink-painted fingernails.

I finally found a seat and watched out of the window as Jazz came running to the bus stop in that all-arms-and-legs way she has, her bag slapping against her back. My heart lurched: my funny friend looked like a multicoloured flamingo. I tapped on the window and waved to her and she looked up and beamed, mouthing something I couldn't make out through the glass. Then I saw her board the bus and start down the aisle towards me. On the way, someone (pretty obvious who . . .) stuck out a long leg and tripped her up. There was some stifled giggling as Jazz picked herself up and looked crossly round to see who the culprit had been.

'Oh hi, Charlie!' she said, switching from hot and bothered to playing it cool. 'Did you see who tripped me?' she added.

'*Tripped* you?' Charlie repeated, making a big

show of sounding puzzled. 'No one tripped you, *Jazz*. You fell. You should be careful, girl. You might *break* something.'

Kez tittered at her friend's hilarious comment.

Jazz blushed, said, 'Yeah. OK. See ya,' and made her way to me. 'Did *you* see someone trip me?' she asked as she sat down. 'I could have sworn someone did.'

I shot a surreptitious glance down the bus and saw that Charlie had turned round in her seat and was staring at me, so I made an effort to smile at Jazz and said, 'I'm not sure. Hey, don't worry about it.'

Jazz spent the rest of the journey prattling on about her *Cat's Eye* programme idea while I pretended to listen. In reality I was keeping a very close eye on Kezia and Charlie. I saw them giggling and looking over their shoulders in our direction as they left the bus, but Jazz was too busy chattering to notice them.

Then, just as the bus pulled up to our stop, it happened.

Beep!

I gulped. My throat was dry. Was this *the* text?

Jazz fished in her bag and pulled out her phone as we staggered to the front. Her face screwed up in concentration as she fumbled to retrieve the message and then read it.

'Who's this then?' she muttered as she saw it was an unknown number. Then 'Oh!' she gasped. She almost dropped the phone as if it was burning hot. I could not breathe. Turning to me she whispered, 'Oh. My. Goodness. This is, like, totally unbelievable.' She clumsily turned the phone round so that the screen was facing me and I read:

Hey, babe! Danni here. Gotta idea for kool new show. Call me!

I read it, then focused all my energy on getting off the bus without falling over. I felt as if all the blood had drained from my head. Pins and needles tingled all over my body.

We stood on the pavement as the bus pulled away, Jazz staring at me, her eyes popping out of her face. Her usually smooth brown face was blotchy with shock and excitement.

'How did she get my number?' she breathed finally. Then, before I could think of anything to say, she answered her own question. 'Fiona!' she said, a smile slowly lighting up her face. 'I gave it to Fiona in the summer when we were doing *PWT*. She must have passed it on to Danni. This is amazing, Bertie!' she babbled. 'It's like Danni's read my mind or something.'

'Jazz,' I began hesitantly 'I agree it's unbelievable. Like, way *too* unbelievable, if you think about it. Don't you reckon it's a bit of a coincidence that you come up with an idea one morning and that very same day you get a text out of the blue? And, well, I'm not sure Danni would spell "cool" like that.'

Jazz was pulling a face. 'What are you saying, Bertie?' she said irritably. 'That this is a *fake* text? Well, why don't I give her a call right now and we'll find out, won't we?'

'NO!' I shouted, putting a hand out to stop her.

'What do you mean, *no*?' she demanded, her expression darkening. 'What's the matter with you? Are you jealous or something?' Her jaw was set and her eyes flashed angrily. I knew better than to try to answer that question. Once Jazz had flared up, it was best to stay quiet. 'Yeah, that's it, isn't it? You *are* jealous!' she went on. '*You* are jealous of *me* because of so many things. For a start, I've got Cupid. So now little Bertie is not the only one with her own gorgeous pussycat. And now my absolute idol wants to do a TV show with me as well – *just me*. This is too much for you, isn't it? Well, you know what? That's not very supportive of you, is it? After everything I did for you when you were on *PWT*.

I thought you were my best mate!' she spluttered. Then, jamming her phone into her pocket, she stuck her chin in the air and stomped off in the direction of her house.

I was so hurt by what she had just said that I did something I regretted afterwards. I just stood and watched her go, the tears welling in my eyes.

When I got home Dad was there, but I hardly stopped to say hello. I rushed to my room, sobs choking me. All I wanted was a cuddle with my kitten and a chance to think straight.

Luckily Dad was tapping away at his computer, and when I rushed past his door, he called out, 'Be with you in a minute – just finishing something!'

I shut my bedroom door behind me and flopped on to my bed head first, burying my face in my pillow. Jaffa had been lying across my desk when I came in, and I heard her jump down lightly and come padding across to nuzzle me gently.

'Why Bertie sleepin'?' she mewed softly in my ear. 'Bertie been out aaaall day and Jaffsie missed her. Bertie not sleeeep now,' she miaowed.

Her little whiskers tickled my ear, making me twitch. I sat up, rubbing my eyes and gulping back the last of my tears.

'What is the wet stuff that is comin' out of Bertie's eyes?' Jaffa asked, rubbing her head against me and purring loudly. 'Has Bertie been swimmin'?'

I let slip a shaky laugh and said, 'No, Bertie has not been swimming. I'm just upset, that's all.'

Jaffa sat back on her haunches and put her head on one side. Then she lifted one dainty paw and washed it carefully, splaying her tiny pink toes and nibbling in between them. When she had finished I took a deep breath and told her what I had heard that day in the loos and what had happened after Jazz had received the text from Kezia.

Jaffa listened thoughtfully, occasionally giving her fur a quick lick. I smiled, remembering that cats liked to 'think before they acted, and wash before they thought', as Kaboodle used to say.

'So what should I do, Jaffsie?'

Jaffa closed her eyes briefly and reached her head forward to touch my face with her nose in a kitten-kiss. Then she opened her eyes wide, their sparkling blue colour giving me that electric shock of love again. 'Jaffsie thinks Bertie should definitely talk to the Fergus,' she said firmly. 'A bully must be put in its place. Jaffsie knows, cos of that nasty Big Bad Bob Cat. It be *much* better if only Jaffsie had told Bertie about him in the first place,' she said, putting her head on one side and looking up at me seriously. 'Me knows that now. And Bertie must tell the prawn lady too,' she added after a moment's hesitation. 'Cos she is a lady who *always* knows what to do.'

I smiled again and stroked the top of her tiny head, listening to her purring. She might have been a baby still, but she was one smart cookie.

I texted Fergus to find out what time he'd be back from band practice, then raced through an early tea with Dad, saying I had a project I needed Fergus's help with.

'OK, just don't stay over there too late, will you? It is a school night,' Dad reminded me unnecessarily. He looked at me over the top of his glasses. (He always does that when he's trying to be firm with me; he thinks it makes him look more impressive.)

'Sure,' I said.

'Bertie will come home and tell Jaffsie what the Fergus says?' my kitten asked, winding in and out of my legs.

I bent down and picked her up. 'Of course,' I whispered, rubbing my nose in her velvety soft fur.

Then I slipped on my trainers and let myself out.

I was in a world of my own as I crossed the road to number 15, wondering what I would say to Fergus, so I jumped out of my skin when the large grey and white cat seemed to appear from nowhere.

'Whaaa!' I screamed, leaping in surprise as he launched himself at me and miaowed in a gruff voice, 'Just the person I wanted to see!'

'Bob!' I said through gritted teeth. 'As always you have perfect timing – not.'

He narrowed his huge yellow eyes and growled, 'The name's Cupid, as you well know, and you can cut the sarky tone, Frizz-ball, and listen to me. My babe and I have got serious problems and, though it pains me to say this, you are the only one I can think of who'll be able to help.'

He jumped up on to the low wall that ran around the Meerleys' front garden and rubbed his head against my arm. 'Just so as we're clear, I'm only

doing this so we look normal to any passers-by, gottit?'

'Eh?'

Cupid gave an impatient hiss. 'I'm be'avin' like any normal pussycat, all right? I'm not schmoozing up to you nor nothin'. It's just so as you don't look like a total lunatic standin' out here talking to me. Blimey, you are hard work,' he ended irritably.

'OK, "Cut the sarky tone," as you would say,' I snapped. 'Tell me what's going on with Jazz. I've been worried sick about her, as it happens. I was just going to talk to Fergus about it.'

'Mm, not sure what help that floppy drip will be,' Cupid growled. And before I could protest, he added quickly, 'It's the Morrises. They've found out where I am. Or they will have done before too long . . . I overheard Jazzie's mum talking to some-one about it on the blower.'

'The Morrises? Oh, your *real* family. The family who knows you as *Bob*, in fact,' I said.

The large cat suddenly looked so incredibly fierce I thought he might bite me or something, so I hastily added a pathetic, 'Oh dear.'

'Oh dear indeed,' Cupid said, dramatically arching his back.

'So when are they coming to collect you?' I asked.

'I dunno . . . yet,' he replied. 'Apparently one of your nosy-parker neighbours saw a poster and recognized the description as being of my good self. They called the Morrises and left a message with 'em and then phoned my Jazzie's mum to say they should expect a call from my rightful owners any day now. My babe's gonna be 'eartbroken,' he added sorrowfully.

'Yes,' I said. This made an urgent situation even worse. Not only was Jazz being bullied, she was about to lose her beloved Cupid kitty-cat too. I had to talk to Fergus. I cast a glance at his house and said, 'Can I go now?'

'Nah, mate,' growled the cat. 'You can't go. You're gonna talk to these Morris people and tell 'em I don't wanna live with 'em no more, got it? They treated me like muck and then ran off and left me, didn't they? They've no right to take me away from my Jazzie.'

I rolled my eyes. 'Look, I'm flattered, really I am, but what am I going to say? "Hello, Mr and Mrs Morris. My name's Bertie Fletcher. I've been talking to your moggie. I'm terribly sorry but he's found himself a new home." They'd have me locked up for being a loony quicker than you could say fish supper!'

'Maybe I didn't make myself clear,' said Cupid, inching closer and giving me the evil eye. 'If you know what's good for you, sunshine, you are gonna sort this out. All right?'

'OK! OK! I'll see what I can do,' I cried, edging towards the door of number 15. 'Gotta dash now!' And eyeing Cupid cautiously, I made a run for it and rang the bell before he could decide to sink his claws into me.

Fergus greeted me with his usual massive grin. 'What's with all the drama, Bert?' he asked teasingly. Then, looking over my shoulder, he said, 'Hey – did you know Jazz's cat had followed you? Look, he's on the wall—'

'Yeah, I know,' I said. 'I couldn't get rid of him. He such an attention-seeker.'

'Oi! I 'eard that!'

'Shut the door quick before he comes in here,' I pleaded, ducking out of Cupid's sight.

I followed Fergus into the kitchen as he chuckled about how it was typical that Jazz had fallen for an attention-seeking cat.

'It's Jazz I need to talk to you about actually,' I said abruptly.

Fergus caught the note of unease in my voice and stopped laughing. 'Oh?' he said. 'What's up?'

'Everything.' I tipped my head back and stared

at the ceiling. 'Looks like Jazz is going to have to give that cat back to his owners after all. But something much worse has happened. At school. I'm not sure if you're going to believe me, cos I know you're friends with them and everything, but—'

'Hey, hey!' said Fergus, putting a hand on my arm and looking concerned. 'Slow down. Start from the beginning.'

So I did. I told him about the overheard conversation, about the fake text, about the audition that never was, and about how I'd been suspicious of the Gruesome Twosome ever since they had first jeered at Jazz that time on the bus.

Fergus listened in silence, his expression growing darker and more serious the more information I gave him. I forced myself to carry on, although a low-level nagging in my brain was telling me that he might never talk to me again after this.

I finished and waited for him to say something. Anything.

But he just carried on staring at me, his face grim. And then Fiona walked in.

'My, don't you two look severe!' she chirruped. 'Not had a tiff, I hope?'

Fergus flicked her a look of disdain – not something I'd ever seen him do before, that was for sure! Then he said, 'Yeah, well, you'd look "severe" if a mate had just ruined your day.'

My blood stopped pumping in my veins. This was it; he was going to tell me to get out. I swallowed hard.

But then he said, 'I think we need your help, Mum. And fast.'

20

Fiona to the Rescue

Relief flooded through me. He was not angry with me, I realized; he believed every word I had told him.

As he spoke, Fiona seemed to steadily work her way up to boiling point. Her carefully made-up face lost all its usual glow, and she grew paler and paler before a tiny spot of red rose on each cheek. When at last Fergus had finished speaking, Fiona hissed like a steaming kettle. I jumped, and even Fergus took a step back.

'This. Is. Appalling,' she spat. 'Firstly, to think that those horrible little girls would play with poor Jasmeena's feelings in this way, and secondly, that

they would involve as talented a celebrity as Danni Minnow . . . This hoax is the sort of thing that could tarnish Danni's name! We must put those minxes in their place right away,' she said decisively. Her dark blue eyes glinted with fury. 'Leave it to me,' she said, drawing herself up to her full height and flicking her shiny mane of hair. She trotted out of the room, her heels clicking on the kitchen tiles, as crisp, impressive and efficient as ever.

Fergus smiled, a hint of menace in his expression. 'You can relax now, Bertie. Now Mum's on the case, Kezia won't know what's hit her.'

I smiled nervously.

Fiona was a fast worker: I'd seen that from the way she had organized Nev's 'surveillance operation'. But even that didn't prepare me for the way she was now attacking this new problem with all guns blazing.

She came back into the room moments later and ordered Fergus to call Jazz. 'No offence, Bertie

darling, but after the misunderstanding you had with her earlier, I think it's best if Fergus gets in touch, don't you?'

I nodded meekly. I was only too willing to let Fiona take control of things, if it meant Jazz would come out on top of this awful situation.

Fergus called the Brown household and sweet-talked Jazz's mum into letting him and his mum go round to talk to Jazz. Apparently Jazz had barricaded herself into her room, and Mrs Brown was not impressed by her daughter's behaviour. 'If you or your mum can talk any sense into her, be my guest, is all I can say,' she told Fergus. 'She's been unbearable for days now. I'm at the end of my tether.'

I tagged along, even though I was secretly quaking in my smelly old trainers at the prospect of Jazz shouting at me again. Cupid was sitting at the bottom of the stairs when we arrived, washing behind his ears. He didn't even look up when we crowded into the hall, only let out a soft growl and said, 'Good on yer, Frizz-ball. Brought in the cavalry, I see.'

Mrs Brown turned at the sound of Cupid's voice and said affectionately, 'He's a big old cutie, that cat.' She looked at me and added, 'I don't know if Jazz has told you the news, but it looks as though Cupid's not going to be staying with us.'

Uh-oh, I thought. So Jazz already knows.

Mrs Brown went on: 'A friend of his owners called today to say she'd seen the poster. She's got their new phone number so she's contacted them. Apparently they lost Cupid while they were packing up the house.'

'Oh,' I said, concentrating on sounding surprised.

'Yes, you can imagine what Jazz's reaction was,' said Mrs Brown. 'I'll be sad to see him go too. He's a real pleasure to have around the place. At least he's pleased to see me when I get home –

unlike some daughters I could mention . . .' she added pointedly.

Fiona patted Jazz's mum on the arm in a gesture which, for her, was comforting. 'You know what, dear, I think you may need to go easy on your daughter.' And she quickly explained about the bullying and how the Gruesome Twosome had tricked Jazz with the non-audition. 'Apparently poor Jasmeena had made a huge effort to impress the two older girls: designed her own outfit, learned a new routine . . .'

Mrs Brown looked horrified.

'I can't believe she didn't tell me this!' she gasped, her hands flying to her face. 'My poor Jazz! No wonder she was in such a strop at the weekend.'

Fiona calmly went on to outline her plan. Then, at her suggestion, Fergus went upstairs to fetch Jazz. There were muffled voices and then a sullen Jazz emerged at the top of the stairs, her face tear-streaked, her eyes red raw. A lump rose in my throat.

We sat in the Browns' sitting room for what seemed like hours as Fiona took Jazz off in private. Mrs Brown kept asking me what I had known about the bullying, and she paced up and down the room, biting her nails and berating herself for not finding out the details sooner. It was horrible.

At last Fiona and Jazz returned. Jazz's puffy face was lit up by a huge grin, her previously teary eyes now sparkly and shining.

'Great news!' announced Fiona, rubbing her hands. 'Jasmeena – won't you tell them?'

Jazz's mum, Fergus and I listened agog, as Jazz breathlessly confirmed that the text had been a fake. 'You were right not to trust it, Bertie,' she said apologetically. 'I don't know how you knew, but you were right. Fiona just called Danni and asked her if she had texted me. She hadn't. When I called the number back, I got Kezia's voicemail.'

I looked away guiltily. 'S'OK,' I mumbled.

Inside I was thinking, 'Ha! What a numpty, leaving her voicemail on! Not so clever now, are we, Kez?'

'But everything's going to be great!' Jazz was saying, flinging her arms around me. 'Fiona told Danni everything. She was horrified that I'd been . . . well . . . bullied.'

'And?' I asked, leaning forward.

'This is the best bit . . .' Jazz paused for dramatic effect, her dark brown eyes shining. I felt like one of the contestants on *Who's Got Talent?*, waiting to find out if I'd been voted off. 'You're not going to believe it, Bertie – *Danni's coming to school*!'

I glanced at Fiona, who nodded curtly (but I couldn't help noticing her cheeks had gone pink with pleasure). 'That's right. She's agreed to help Jasmeena set the record straight.'

'How?' I asked, impatient to know the details.

'Danni Minnow is going to come in and give a talk about her life and career IN FRONT OF THE WHOLE SCHOOL! And I am going to get to look after her! I cannot WAIT to see the look on Kezia's face.'

'I have already spoken to the Head,' Fiona said, 'and I told him that Danni will call him this evening to arrange it. He was thrilled, as you can imagine. What man *wouldn't* be thrilled to get a call from a top celebrity as beautiful and talented as Danni Minnow?' She raised a perfectly plucked eyebrow and grinned mischievously. 'I think you'll find he'd move heaven and earth, not to mention the school timetable, to fit in a visit from an international superstar.'

'Fiona!' said Jazz's mum in mock shock.

'Wow.' I shook my head in genuine admiration.

'Wow indeed,' said Fiona. 'There is one thing, though. May I make a suggestion?'

We all nodded. After what she had just told us, she could suggest we all dress as monkeys and swing from the light fittings as far as I was concerned.

'I think it would be better to keep the visit a

secret from Kezia and her little friends until Danni arrives in person. What do you say, Jasmeena?' Her eyes twinkled wickedly.

'Yaaaaahoooooooooo!' Jazz bellowed. She launched herself at Fiona, practically knocking her off balance, and flung her arms around her.

Fiona's eyebrows shot up into her fringe and I had a ghastly sick feeling that she was going to shout at Jazz to get off. But all at once her face broke into a huge grin and she gave my funny friend a big squeeze back.

'I'm pleased you like the idea,' Fiona said, regaining her composure as Jazz released her.

'LIKE it?' Jazz squealed. 'It's an idea of total and utter genius-ness! *You* are a genius, Fiona! I LOVE you!' she yelled, dancing round and round in circles, whooping and punching the air. Tyson rushed in to see what all the noise was about and joined in the victory dance, adding to the general hullabaloo.

Cupid came padding in too. He nudged me

with his head and miaowed, 'You sorted it then, Frizz-ball?'

I bent down and was going to say that I hadn't yet had a chance, but Jazz was too quick for me. She picked him up and said sadly, 'If only the Morrises don't call. Then all my dreams will come true.'

We stood around awkwardly, making sympathetic noises, not knowing what to say. Cupid shot a beady-eyed sneer in my direction and growled menacingly. I tried to tell him with a tiny shrug that I was out of ideas.

Then Fiona was saying her goodbyes and ordering her son to leave with her. 'Come along, Fergie dear. Your father will wonder what on earth has happened to us.'

As he followed his mum out he mimed a phone with his hand and mouthed, 'Call me later.'

I would, I thought, as I said goodbye. If only to ask for his help in working out a solution to our second problem – how to stop Cupid leaving.

21

Winners and Losers

Fiona's plan (code name: Operation Embarrass the Enemy) went without a hitch. The Head was only too pleased to keep Danni's visit a secret. Apparently he told Fiona he would have 'mass hysteria' on his hands if he announced her arrival too early on.

'Better that I tell the school there will be a special assembly at the end of the day. I'll say we have a guest speaker coming – we have had those in the past. No one would ever suspect someone as exciting as Danni Minnow though!' he had chortled. 'We usually get the chief of the Fire Service or someone from the local council.'

So it was arranged that Danni would arrive while we were all in class and wait in the staffroom, out of sight. Meanwhile, Jazz would be given the enviable task of looking after Danni before bringing her to the hall. That would keep her from brooding about Cupid, I thought gratefully.

'How did you persuade the Head to give a Year Seven such an important job?' I asked Fiona.

'Oh, I just mentioned how marvellous Jazz was as Danni's personal assistant when we filmed *Pets with Talent* in the summer,' Fiona said airily. 'He thought it was a fabulous idea to have a pupil introduce the mystery guest. If Jasmeena is to have her moment in the sun, I am determined to make it shine upon her as brightly as possible!' she declared.

Jazz was, of course, bubbling over with excitement. How she managed to keep herself from spilling the beans over the next few days, I have no idea. In fact, she actually kept an incredibly low profile, sticking to me like glue at break and lunch

times, and even getting me to walk with her to and from street dance and music classes.

'All this pretending is great practice for my future career on stage and screen,' she confided in me at one point. 'It's called "character acting" – you know, when you live the life of the character you're trying to portray.'

'But, Jazz, you really and truly *are* the character,' I pointed out. 'In real life.'

'Thank you!' she said, completely misunderstanding me. 'See? I must be getting the hang of it already. Hey, by the way, Cupid's been acting really oddly. He doesn't want to cuddle me so much at the moment. It's almost as if he knows his old owners might come and get him at any minute. I couldn't bear it, you know. I love my little Mr Snuggly toooo much—'

'Yeah,' I cut in hastily, 'I know. Listen, don't worry about it. Cats can be a bit stand-offish like that. Focus on Danni's visit, eh?'

★

Jazz arrived at school on The Day with her hair freshly braided and beaded, and wearing some pretty obvious (and very non-regulation) glittery eye make-up. Her skirt seemed to have shrunk overnight as well.

'You like?' she trilled, waving her fingernails at me. They were false, like the ones she'd worn to try to impress Fergus the first time she'd met him!

I rolled my eyes. 'Yeah, yeah, I like.' Holy moly! How on earth had she got that lot past her mum?

Jazz cackled madly. 'This is the best day of my liiiiiife!' she sang as we danced into school together, arm in arm, ignoring the strange looks from everyone around us.

Danni arrived later that day in her trademark black limo and was greeted outside the gates by Fiona, the Head, Jazz, Fergus and me. As she peeled herself out of the sleek black car, she immediately made eye contact with Jazz and winked. In fact, the

first person she spoke to wasn't Fiona Meerley; it wasn't even the Head. She walked right up to Jazz and threw her long tanned arms around my best friend's neck.

'Hey, chick!' she cooed, kissing Jazz on both cheeks. 'It's awesome to see you again. You look a-maz-ing too in that cute little uniform. I'm *loving* the accessories, girl!' she trilled, running her perfectly manicured hand over Jazz's bangles.

Jazz was so chuffed that for once in her life she was completely and utterly speechless.

'So, show me round, why don't you?' Danni purred, linking her arm through Jazz's and winking at me.

We took Danni into the staff room and made her a coffee while she charmed her way round all the male teachers and amused the female ones by swapping fashion tips and telling them hilarious celebrity anecdotes. Then the bell rang and it was time for the assembly. As Fergus and I went back to our classrooms to leave Jazz to her moment of glory, I found myself thinking about that blinking cat again. It was weird how I had been desperate to see the back of him and yet now, seeing my best friend so happy, chattering away to her idol, I found myself wishing harder than ever that she would be able to keep Cupid. She was right: it *would* mean all her dreams coming true in one fell swoop. And even though I didn't think I would ever be totally cool with being called 'Frizz-ball', there was something about his rascally character that I realized I was beginning to warm to.

I filed into the hall with my class. The atmosphere was the usual: a low hum indicated people were talking quietly as they waited, but they weren't really interested in what they were waiting for. It was obvious by the total lack of enthusiasm that no one suspected a thing. But then, why should they? Assemblies with guest speakers were usually as sleep-inducing as a visit to a hypnotist.

My heart was somewhere in the region of my mouth and was doing a jumpy-hoppy-skippy routine – it was almost enough to make me throw up. I was nervous for Jazz and excited for her at the same time.

A hush descended on the hall as the Head walked on to the stage and did his usual spiel about what a good week we had had and how important it was to keep working and thinking as a team. Then he said:

'And now, I am absolutely thrilled to introduce our guest speaker. She is a lady who is no stranger to hard work and I'm sure she'll inspire you the way she's inspired millions of others already with her gift and talent for music and her determination to succeed. Please put your hands together to welcome . . . *Who's Got Talent?*'s DANNI MINNOW!'

There was silence.

'Did he just say *Danni Minnow*?' a girl in front

of me whispered. A gasp rippled around the hall like a Mexican wave and then, I don't know what came over me, I shouted, 'Whoooo!' and stood up and clapped and cheered. Thankfully the people around me immediately leaped up too, and soon the whole school was cheering and stamping their feet.

At that moment Danni appeared from the wings of the stage, holding hands with Jazz! My friend was beaming so widely from ear to ear it looked as though her face might actually split in two. When the kids realized a pupil was up there on stage with Danni, the cheering and whooping started to die down and people began to whisper to one another curiously.

'Hey, everyone!' Danni called out in her famous drawl. The whispering went up a notch, and Jazz's grin began to fade. I gulped. 'I *said*, "Hey, everyone!"' Danni repeated, lifting one hand up to the ceiling. Immediately there was a roar of 'Hey,

Danni!' in response. Then Danni said, 'And I want you all to say hi to my friend Jazz. She and I met this summer on the show *Pets with Talent*. Some of you may have seen it – great, wasn't it?' Calls of 'Yeah' and 'Great' went up around the hall. Danni nodded and continued, 'Well, Jazz was my personal assistant for the whole time I was working on the show, and she was without doubt the best, most fun and funky person I've ever worked with. So, let's hear it for Jazz!'

The school bellowed out a massive 'Jaa-aazz! Jaa-aazz!'

My best mate's cheeks flushed with pleasure. She smiled gratefully at Danni, who promptly enveloped her in a tight hug and kissed her.

Jazz left Danni to her talk after that. She had everyone riveted with her story of how she had made it from rags to riches and what life as a top celebrity was really like behind the scenes: apparently not all fun and laughter. Although I don't think much of that part of the story got through to Danni's besotted fans.

But the audience wasn't so hooked on Danni's talk that they'd forgotten about Jazz. As she pushed past people to come and sit with me, everyone turned and looked at her and whispered and waved. It wasn't the first time Jazz had turned heads at our new school, but this time instead of everyone enjoying nasty rumours about her, they wanted to show her how cool they thought she was. I grinned at her and gave her hand a squeeze. 'You're a real star now, Jazz!' I told her.

'Thank you!' she mouthed, her eyes shining with happy tears.

After the talk Danni was signing autographs and chatting with people, when Jazz, Fergus and I went to thank her.

'Awwww, chicks! It was nothing,' she cooed. 'When Fiona told me you'd been bullied, Jazz,

I sooo had to do something. You're a gorgeous babe – and you're my friend. And no one messes with Danni's friends,' she added, faking a mean face.

'Er, hi,' said a voice behind us.

'Kezia!' I breathed as Jazz whirled round to come face to face with her enemy.

Danni held out one elegant hand and, fixing Kezia with a barbed smile, she said, 'Great to meet you, chick. And I think you know my good friends here?'

'Yeah, er . . . ace talk,' Kezia mumbled. 'I was wondering, like, er . . . could I have a photo with you?' she asked shyly, waving her phone limply.

'Sorry, babe,' said Danni. 'I only do photos with *close friends*.' She winked at Jazz and draped a protective arm around her.

I held my breath as a dark storm gathered across Kezia's features. She wouldn't talk back to Danni, surely?

But, flicking Jazz an awkward glance, Kezia

turned quickly on her heel and scuttled off.

'Ha!' said Jazz, punching the air in victory. 'Jazz one, Kezia NIL!'

'You make sure that's the way it stays, girl,' said Danni, giving her a squeeze.

Epilogue
Kitten Cupid

And thankfully, that *was* the way it stayed. Jazz went home that day on a massive high, to find out that not only had she won one over on the bullies, but Cupid was hers for keeps.

'Seems those Morrises can't come and get me,' he told me later. 'Can't or won't, more like . . . They've moved to the other side of the world, would yer believe it? To a place called "Ors-trail-ya" or summin. And they 'ad the audacity to tell my Jazzie's mum that my babe was welcome to me, cos as far as they were concerned I was a thug and a bully. Would yer credit it?'

I bit my lip. 'Noooo,' I said with barely

concealed sarcasm. 'How could anyone say that about a cute little heartbreaker like you, Cupid?'

Life really did calm down immensely once Jazz had got what she wanted.

'You've got nothing to worry about now, Jaffsie,' I told my little kitten once I had filled her in on the day's excitement. 'Cupid is so comfy in his new home that there is no way he'll be coming round here any more.'

'Well, me is relieved 'bout that, me can tell you,' Jaffsie said, snuggling into my lap.

Dad was pleased things had all been sorted too. 'Perhaps we can have a bit of peace and quiet around here now,' he said that night at supper. 'What with all your pet-sitting nonsense getting you into trouble, and then adopting Jaffa – only to find she kept running off – and then this breaking-and-entering stuff with Cupid . . . you must admit that life's been more than a little "cat-astrophic" – ha ha haa!' He laughed uproariously at his own pathetic joke.

'Tee-hee!' Bex joined in. 'Oh, you are funny, Nigel,' she cooed, leaning into him for a hug.

I rolled my eyes, but inside I was actually glowing. My best mate was happy again, my kitten was safe and my dad was beaming like a chimp who's won the banana lottery on a rollover week.

If I had any worries at all, it was that once the excitement had faded Jazz might move on to her next crazy project, i.e. begging Fiona to let her do her *Cat's Eye* programme. But luckily for all of us, Jazz's bonkers idea had evaporated into thin air and was not mentioned again.

'Maybe she learned her lesson,' Fergus said when we were discussing it one day after school. 'I mean, if she hadn't got involved in the *Pets with Talent* thing, she never would have been picked on by Kez.'

'Yeah, that and the fact that she's so lurrrrrved up with Cupid. She *is* pretty distracted these days.' I sniggered.

Fergus stared at the ground and shuffled his feet. 'Yeah, everyone seems kind of paired up these days, in a way,' he said carelessly.

'What d'you mean?' I shot back.

'Well, there's Jazz and Cupid, your dad and Bex and, er . . . yeah . . .' He tailed off.

'Hmm,' I said thoughtfully.

It was true: Dad and Bex were definitely an item now, there was no denying it. Bex was round at our place more often than not. But somehow it had happened so naturally that I hadn't really noticed. And now that I *had* noticed, I realized that I was totally cool with it.

'So, like, d'you want to go to the cinema on Friday?' Fergus said in a rush, still staring at the floor.

'Er, yes,' I said, finding the floor rather interesting myself, all of a sudden.

Well, what d'you know?
Life never stops being full
of surprises, does it?

A Message from the Author

'Where do you get your inspiration from?'

Whenever I tell people I am a writer, this is what they often ask me. Some people seem to think that inspiration is a special kind of magic that comes to writers out of thin air while they are sitting at their desk, staring at a blank screen or a clean sheet of paper. But the answer is actually much more straightforward than that: inspiration comes from watching and noting down what happens around you in your life.

When I finished *Kitten Smitten* I wanted to write another story about Bertie and Jaffa. For ideas, I thought back over the various adventures that my cats, Inky and Jet, have been through in the five years they have been living with us. Now, as those of you with pets will know, funny things happen all the time when you are living with animals. And sometimes scary things too . . .

When Inky and Jet were still quite small, a scary thing happened to them. They were bullied, just like Jaffa is in *Kitten Cupid*, by a bigger, tougher cat. At the time, we lived near a couple of farms, and some of the cats on those farms were pretty frightening beasts – not at all like my pampered moggies. If you are a farm cat you sometimes have to fend for yourself and, er, get your *own* dinner, if you know what I mean, and that can make you into a bit of a toughie. The cats in our neighbourhood could be really fierce, and it wasn't long before one of these menaces found out that he could 'break and enter' our house through the cat flap. He was soon tucking into Jet and Inky's food, using our utility room as if it was a drive-through takeaway restaurant! And did Jet or Inky put up a fight when the intruder appeared? Not a bit of it! They were far too worried about what he would do to them, and always hid whenever the bully appeared.

In the end I got fed up with putting out food only to find it had been gobbled up by the Bully Cat, so I lay in wait for him one evening. He usually scarpered before I managed to get hold of him, but this time I just sat and waited quietly. I needed to teach that cat a lesson he would not forget . . .

He normally crashed in around teatime, and sure enough he arrived on the dot, the minute I had put the food out. I waited until he was face down in the cat dish, guzzling and chomping away, then I crept up behind him and –

SPLASH! I chucked the entire contents of a watering can all over him! My children thought it was very cruel, but he never came back – and anyway, I reckoned he deserved a soaking for being such a meanie to my own cats.

So that is where I got my inspiration for Bob/Cupid: of course I changed the story to create what I hope is a funnier tale – and one with a kinder and happier ending!

There is one other element of *Kitten Cupid* which comes from a true experience: Inky really did force her way through a locked cat flap. We had shut her into the house to stop her from running off, because she had to go to the vet the next morning and she always seems to have a sixth sense about this. She has been known to disappear for the whole day when she's due to go, and this time we were not taking any chances.

The next morning, when it was time to put her in the cat box, we opened the utility-room door to find the cat flap hanging from its hinges, the locks broken and clumps of black fur and smears of blood around the edges. We were so worried – we thought the Bully Cat might have come back or that, even worse, a fox or badger might have got in and terrorized Inky. We spent all day looking for her to no avail.

Finally, at the end of the day, Inky appeared in the garden, cool as an ice pop, with a look on her face as if to say, 'You didn't really think you could fool me, did you?'

We had the last laugh though – she had to go to the vet right away because she had a small cut on her head from the broken cat flap and she needed antibiotics as well as the injections we had booked her in for in the first place! Daft cat.

If you would like to know any more stories about my pets, or if you have any questions for me, why not take a look at my website: www.annawilson.co.uk, or my blog: www.annawilsonbarkingmad.blogspot.com, where you can leave me a comment. And if you would like to write to me, you can email me at: annawilson@macmillan.co.uk, or send a letter to:

Anna Wilson
c/o Macmillan Children's Books
20 New Wharf Road
London
N1 9RR

Love

Anna
xxx

PS Don't forget to enclose a stamped addressed envelope if you want me to return any pictures you send me!

A Message from the Illustrator

If you love drawing, I hope that one day you'll be as lucky as I am, and get to illustrate a book for Anna Wilson. Here's what she wrote when she saw my little kitten drawings: 'Oh oh oh ooooohhhhhh! They are GORGEOOOOOOUU-UUUUS!' and 'Scrum-diddly-umptious!' I think Anna Wilson is actually Mary Poppins in disguise.

Moira Munro

Kitten Kaboodle

Anna Wilson

Bertie Fletcher's Pet-sitting Service is open for business!

Lonely Bertie has only ever wanted one thing – a pet – but her grumpy dad won't even let her have a goldfish. So she secretly sets up her own pet-sitting business – and meets Kaboodle, the tiny kitten who lives across the road . . .

A funny, heart-warming and slightly cat-astrophic story about a kitten whose tongue is sharper than his claws!

Kitten Smitten

Anna Wilson

What happens when two families are smitten by the same kitten?

With new pet Jaffa in her life, Bertie Fletcher is happier than the cat that got the custard. But then the annoyingly perfect Meerley family arrives on the scene and threatens to lure 'Muffin' away in a dramatic tug of love. May the best family win . . .

A hilariously zany story about a cat with too many owners on her paws!

Monkey Business

Anna Wilson

It's so BORING having normal pets!

For Felix and Flo, animals are the NUMBER ONE TOP PRIORITY in life. And although Felix loves his pets (a lazy dog, an angry cat and a noisy hamster), what he really wants is to look after an animal which is EXOTIC and DIFFERENT. Will Flo's brilliant and FOOLPROOF plan get Felix his perfect pet – or will it just send him bananas?

A side-splittingly chaotic story about schemes, dreams and monkeying around.

Coming soon to all good bookshops!

A selected list of titles available from Macmillan Children's Books

The prices shown below are correct at the time of going to press. However, Macmillan Publishers reserves the right to show new retail prices on covers, which may differ from those previously advertised.

Anna Wilson

KITTEN KABOODLE	978-0-330-50771-4	£4.99
KITTEN SMITTEN	978-0-330-50772-1	£4.99
PUPPY LOVE	978-0-330-45289-2	£4.99
PUP IDOL	978-0-330-45290-8	£5.99
PUPPY POWER	978-0-330-45291-5	£4.99

Chosen by Anna Wilson

FAIRY STORIES	978-0-330-43823-0	£4.99
PRINCESS STORIES	978-0-330-43797-4	£4.99